RAVE REVIEWS FOR BARBARA LEBOW'S
A SHAYNA MAIDEL

"In A SHAYNA MAIDEL, two sisters—one a survivor of Nazi concentration camps, the other brought up as an American— meet in 1946 after a separation of almost 20 years, and in the course of a heartrending evening, they achieve an intimacy that transcends the theatrical event. Barbara Lebow's play is about the horrors of the Holocaust; it is also a deeply personalized study of sisterhood, family and a crisis of faith."
—Mel Gussow, *The New York Times*

"Lebow's play has the effect high tragedy is said to produce: you weep and weep and emerge from the theatre feeling uplifted without knowing why."   —*The New Yorker*

"Moving. Searing. Shattering. The most powerful statement about Holocaust survival and its aftermath I have ever seen. Yet it isn't a Holocaust play. A SHAYNA MAIDEL is a universal drama. It is a testimony to the power of theater and the genius of a single playwright. . . . It deserves the epithet masterpiece."
—*The Jewish Journal*

BARBARA LEBOW, a New Yorker by birth, currently lives in Atlanta, Georgia, where she is playwright-in-residence at the Academy Theater. She is the author of twenty plays, two of which have been cited in the *Best Plays* yearbook.

A
SHAYNA MAIDEL

by BARBARA LEBOW

A PLUME BOOK

NEW AMERICAN LIBRARY

NEW YORK AND SCARBOROUGH, ONTARIO

PLUME TRADEMARK REG. U.S. PAT. OFF. AND FOREIGN COUNTRIES
REGISTERED TRADEMARK—MARCA REGISTRADA
HECHO EN CHICAGO, U.S.A.

SIGNET, SIGNET CLASSIC, MENTOR, ONYX, PLUME, MERIDIAN
and NAL BOOKS are published *in the United States* by
NAL PENGUIN INC., 1633 Broadway, New York, New York 10019,
in Canada by The New American Library of Canada Limited,
81 Mack Avenue, Scarborough, Ontario M1L 1M8

Library of Congress Cataloging-in-Publication Data

Lebow, Barbara.
A shayna maidel / by Barbara Lebow.
p. cm.
ISBN 0-452-26150-3
1. Holocaust, Jewish (1939–1945)—Drama.
PS3562.E2648S53 1988
812'54—dc19   88-5319
                                                                CIP

First Printing, September, 1988

1 2 3 4 5 6 7 8 9

PRINTED IN THE UNITED STATES OF AMERICA

A SHAYNA MAIDEL was first produced at the Academy Theatre's First Stage New Play Series, April 18, 1985. The script was completed during the Academy Theatre's Mainstage production, April 9, 1986, with the following cast:

ROSE WEISS	*Mary Jo Ammon*
MORDECHAI WEISS	*Frank Wittow*
LUSIA WEISS PECHENIK	*Shawna McKellar*
DUVID PECHENIK	*Daniel Reichard*
HANNA	*Ruth Reid*
MAMA	*Margaret Ferguson*

Production Staff:
Director: Barbara Lebow
Set Design: Michael Halpern
Lighting Design: Richard Johnson
Costume Design: Judy Winograd
Stage Manager: Chris Kayser
Voices Design: Phillip DePoy

A SHAYNA MAIDEL was subsequently presented at the Hartford Stage Company (Mark Lamos, Artistic Director; David Hawkanson, Managing Director) in Hartford, Connecticut, in November, 1985. It was directed by Robert Kalfin; the production design was by Wolfgang Roth; the costume design was by Eduardo Sicangco; the lighting design was by Curt Ostermann; the sound design was by David Budries; the stage manager was Alice Dewey; and the casting was by Stanley Soble and Jason LaPadura. The cast was as follows:

ROSE WEISS	*Lindsey Margo Smith*
MORDECHAI WEISS	*Mark Margolis*
LUSIA WEISS PECHENIK	*Gordana Rashovich*
DUVID PECHENIK	*Ray Dooley*
HANNA	*Kate Fuglei*
MAMA	*Maggie Burke*

A SHAYNA MAIDEL was subsequently presented at the Hartford Stage Company (Mark Lamos, artistic Director; David Hawkanson, Managing Director) in Hartford, Connecticut, in November, 1985. It was directed by Robert Kalfin, the production design was by Wolfgang Roth, the costume design was by Eduardo Sicango, the lighting design was by Gary Ostennan; the sound design was by David Budries; the stage manager was Nina Dewey; and the casting was by Stanley Soble and Elissa LaPadula. The cast was as follows:

ROSE WEISS .... Linda ? Sharon Singer
MORDECHAI WEISS .... Mark Mazurki
LUSIA WEISS PECHENIK .... Giulanna Richardson
DUVID PECHENIK .... Roy Dooley
HANNA .... Karel Pagliaro
MAMA .... Maggie Burke

A SHAYNA MAIDEL was presented by K&D Productions, Margery Klain and Robert G. Donnalley, Jr., at the Westside Arts Theatre (under the direction of Raymond L. Gaspard) in New York City on October 29, 1987. It was directed by Mary B. Robinson; the set design was by William Barclay; the costume design was by Mimi Maxmen; the lighting design was by Dennis Parichy; the sound design was by Aural Fixation; the associate producer was Susan Urban Horsey; the casting was by David Tochterman; the production stage manager was Crystal Huntington; the general management was Darwall Associates. The cast, in order of appearance, was as follows:

ROSE WEISS	*Melissa Gilbert*
MORDECHAI WEISS	*Paul Sparer*
LUSIA WEISS PECHENIK	*Gordana Rashovich*
DUVID PECHENIK	*Jon Tenney*
HANNA	*Cordelia Richards*
MAMA	*Joan MacIntosh*

PLAYWRIGHT'S NOTES

When memory or fantasy create a time or place other than Rose Weiss's apartment, this is indicated by changes in the lighting. Music may also be used to parenthesize fantasies. Imagined characters should appear realistically within scenes, not be removed by scrims or other illusions. However, they may enter from outside the realistic entrances on the set.

At times throughout the play, there can be an interweaving of one or more disembodied *voices* with the action of the play. Usually there is only a suggestion of acknowledgment, a look, a slight hesitation, by the actors since the sounds are internal, rather than external, reflections of feelings and memory. Whatever sounds, human or other, are used for these voices are recognizably related, growing from the same line, Mama's lullaby, since they form a continuum of awareness.

The action of the play occurs *before* and *after* time lived in the camps. It is important that any references to life and death in the camps be filled in by the audience. There should be no visual or auditory images suggesting a concentration camp. Any temptation to play tragedy, sentiment, or melodrama, must be avoided at all costs. The characters should be perceived by actors and director simply as members of a family who cannot communicate. They do not know the Holocaust is behind them.

Except for Rose, all the characters have a Yiddish accent when they are speaking in English. However, in the memory or fantasy scenes where these characters are assumed to be speaking in Yiddish, the actors should shift into unaccented English. Some Yiddish is used in the play and a glossary is provided of words and phrases not otherwise translated in the text to assist those working on, or reading, the play. In performance, most of the Yiddish dialogue will be understood by a non-Yiddish speaking audience as long as the actors know what they are saying. Spoken, many of the Yiddish words resemble their English translations. Gesture and intonation will help clarify meaning and the words give no important new information. The Yiddish flavor is what matters.

Suggested for Mama's lullaby: *Rozhinkes Mit Mandlen* (traditional).

THE SETTING

Prologue
1876, a small Polish village

Acts I & II
March 1946, Rose Weiss's apartment,
New York City, West Side

CHARACTERS

ROSE WEISS, early 20s
MORDECHAI WEISS, her father, almost 70
LUSIA WEISS PECHENIK, her older sister, late 20s
   (younger in memory scenes)
DUVID PECHENIK, Lusia's husband, 30 (younger in
   memory scenes)
HANNA, a childhood friend of Lusia, age ranges from 14
   to late 20s
MAMA, mother of Rose and Lusia, various ages
MIDWIFE
MOTHER
DAUGHTER
MAN, daughter's husband

*The last four characters appear only in Act I Scene 1 and are
doubled with the other roles.*

A
SHAYNA MAIDEL

Act I

SCENE ONE

The main action of the play takes place in ROSE WEISS*'s*
apartment in New York City in 1946. The living room of the
apartment is Center Stage with raised platforms Stage Left
and Stage Right to serve as bedroom and dinette. There are
doorways which lead from the dinette to the offstage kitchen
and from the bedroom to the offstage bathroom and closet.
Upstage Center an entranceway from the living room leads
off on one side to the bathroom and closet and off on the
other side to the front door. There are no working doors
onstage.

As the play begins, the stage is in darkness. It is 1876 in a
Polish shtetl. *The scene has a dream-like surrealistic quality.*
Illumination of the characters is no more than that from a
single candle. The DAUGHTER, *whom we do not see, but*
whose voice is heard clearly, in labor, is attended by her
MOTHER *and a* MIDWIFE, *dressed in long skirts, with their*
heads covered. Her HUSBAND *wears a prayer shawl. In*
addition to the urgency of the imminent birth, all are fright-
ened of something outside. There are moments when they
freeze, like the moment of suspension when an animal senses
danger. At times these moments are precipitated by some-
thing of which only the characters are aware; sometimes a
distant shout or noise is audible to the audience. Growing
out of the darkness, the first sounds in the scene are the
words of a quietly intoned Hebrew prayer.

3

HUSBAND: *Hashem yish-mereynu mikhol ro veyishmor ses nafsheynu.*
(*This is repeated throughout the scene at a small distance away from the other activities. When the prayer has been established, it is joined by the heavy breathing and muffled cries of the* DAUGHTER.)

MIDWIFE: *Licht. Mir muzn hobn licht!*
(*The single candle is lit. The following lines and actions are spaced and played under the conditions described above.*)

DAUGHTER: Mama! Mama!
(MOTHER *hushes and comforts the* DAUGHTER.)

MOTHER: (*In response to an outside noise.*) Cossacks!
(*Out of one of the silent freezes, a baby begins to cry, creaking like an old door.*)

MIDWIFE: A boy! A blessing on him.
(*The baby is wrapped and held.*)

MOTHER: (*Quieting the infant.*) Sha, my child. Sha, sha.
The baby is quiet.

DAUGHTER: You must tell my husband.

MIDWIFE: Reb Weiss . . .
(*The praying stops for the first time.*)
Reb Weiss, you have a son.

HUSBAND: (*Holding the baby stiffly.*) We shall call him Mordechai.

DAUGHTER: Itzik, look! He already knows not to cry.
(*A sound in the distance. Another frozen moment.*)

MIDWIFE: *Di licht!*
(*She blows out the candle. In the darkness, galloping horses come closer and ride by. Growing out of this sound, and taking over for it as it fades, is a knocking on the door and the loud and insistent ringing of a doorbell.*)

The apartment. Near midnight. The first doorbell ring is followed by intermittent knocking and ringing. Light in the bedroom. ROSE, *awakened, is startled.*

MORDECHAI: *(Offstage.)* Rayzel! Open up the door!

ROSE: Papa?
(She grabs a robe.)

MORDECHAI: Who else? Hurry up, Rayzel! What's taking so long?
(Rose goes to open the front door and returns to the living room, followed by MORDECHAI WEISS. *Though he has been a hard worker all his life,* MORDECHAI *is a dignified and elegant man with an aristocratic look. He carries a cane, used for style and emphasis rather than for aid in walking, since he moves easily. He wears a coat over a well-pressed dark suit. He removes his hat and scarf, automatically gives them to* ROSE, *who puts them down as they begin speaking.)*

ROSE: I was asleep, Papa. What's the matter? It's the middle of the night.

MORDECHAI: *(He has an old-country Yiddish accent, incongruous to his appearance.)* I got big news. Important news. Sit.

ROSE: *(She sits as ordered; speaks to him as she always does, unconsciously picking up some of his inflection.)* Well, what is it, Papa? Tell me. You're scaring me to death.

MORDECHAI: Glass water first, please.
*(*MORDECHAI *sits down, pulling papers from an inside pocket, opening, reading and arranging them as* ROSE

5

goes for water and returns. He sips a little, places the glass down carefully, motions for her to sit again, clears his throat.)
Thanks to God, I found your sister.

ROSE: *(Stunned, speaks softly after a moment.)* My sister! When, Papa? Where? How? How is she?

MORDECHAI: Came these letters from Red Cross and from Hebrew Immigrant Aid Society both together today. To Mr. Mordechai Weiss in Brooklyn.
(Carefully hands papers to ROSE.*)* She went from concentration camp Poland to hospital Sweden. I make lots phone calls from Greenspans' to be sure and I'm down to immigrant office waiting with more people on same kind business. She comes here by boat in three more weeks. Thanks to God they left one from the family alive.

ROSE: I can't believe it.

MORDECHAI: Is truth. From centuries, from cossacks to Hitler *(Ich hob im in drerd!)* they tried to wipe out everybody! But you I got away in time and now your sister . . .

ROSE: *(Reading.)* Lusia Weiss Pechenik? She must be married.

MORDECHAI: A married woman . . . last we seen her she was this big.

ROSE: I don't remember her. Or my mother.

MORDECHAI: Soon you'll remember. When she comes, she'll stay here with you.

ROSE: But Papa, wouldn't it be better if she stayed with you at Greenspans'?

MORDECHAI: If it came out different, maybe. If someone else was saved. If we was going to be a family again, we should all be under one roof. Even you. But it didn't come out different. So, in three weeks from now, you'll take a vacation from work.

ROSE: I just got the position, Papa.

MORDECHAI: The boss, he'll understand. Your sister is more important. They give you any trouble over this big, New York po-si-tion, I'll go myself and talk to them or you'll quit because if they don't see the point, they're no good anyway!

ROSE: I'll work it out, Papa.

MORDECHAI: You got to be with her every minute. Take care like a nurse her health, her sleep, her food, everything.

ROSE: But I don't even know her.

MORDECHAI: Is your flesh and blood.

ROSE: Why can't *Tanta* Perla—

MORDECHAI: Your *Tanta* Perla has a bad foot. She sits all day in a chair on the front porch. Anyway, she done her work with you. Now you take care your sister.
(He stands, putting on hat and scarf.)
Every day I'll come visit.

ROSE: But Papa, the place is so small! There's no room for anyone else.

MORDECHAI: Don't let me hear such a thing!
(He walks around, pointing with his cane as ROSE *tries to get a word in, but can't.)*
Lusia sleeps in there. You here on sofa. Is your flesh and blood. A blessing from God on this family saved her life so no more words from you. Brooklyn's not good enough for you anymore so maybe Brooklyn's not good enough for your sister, too.
(Indicating kitchen with cane.)
And from now on you'll keep kosher like you're sup-posed to, like you was taught.

ROSE: I told you I—

MORDECHAI: Don't tell me nothing. I know what goes on. A hundred percent kosher from this minute. Perfect. Everything like she's used to. I want she should feel at home.

ROSE: But, Papa—

MORDECHAI: *(Overlapping.)* When such a miracle happens and you got now a sister, you don't say the word "but."

ROSE: I know, Papa. I'm really very happy, but we don't know each other. We're strangers.

MORDECHAI: *(Pounding floor with cane.) Shvesters! Ain flaish!* (MORDECHAI *moves toward the front door.)*
I come to the boat with you, three weeks Tuesday. You find out what time, the details. Greenspan can live without me half a day . . . *Gai schlofen*, Rayzel. It's late.
*(*MORDECHAI *exits,* ROSE *grabs the water glass from where he left it and walks quickly toward the kitchen. In the dinette, she stops suddenly. She stands, unmoving. As the light fades to black, the voice of a woman [*MAMA*] is heard singing sweetly in Yiddish: a lullaby.)*

Two-and-a-half weeks later. A Friday near midnight. A phone rings loudly. It rings again. ROSE *is awakened suddenly. Bedroom light rises.*

ROSE: *(Answering phone sleepily.)* Hello.
(In another area of the stage LUSIA *appears, tightly lit. She speaks uncertainly with a very thick Yiddish-Polish accent. Her voice is gentle.)*

LUSIA: Rayzel Weiss.

ROSE: Hello?

LUSIA: Rayzel Weiss.

ROSE: What did you say? Who is this?

LUSIA: I want speak Rayzel Weiss, please you.

ROSE: I think you have the wrong number.
(ROSE is about to hang up, unsure. LUSIA looks helpless and confused.)

LUSIA: Wait, please.

ROSE: Yes?

LUSIA: *(She speaks very slowly.)* I want to speak *mit* mine *shvester.* Rayzel Weiss. Mine *shvester*—sis-ter—Rayzel Weiss.

ROSE: *(Sits up fast. Waits. She speaks tentatively, amazed and frightened.)* Lusia? Is this Lusia?

LUSIA: Lusia Pechenik. Is Lusia Weiss Pechenik.

ROSE: Lusia! This is me. It's Rose. Rayzel. Your sister. Where are you? I didn't expect to hear from you till Tuesday. Where are you calling from?

9

LUSIA: In New York City.
(Reading from a card.)
Hebrew Immigrant Aid Society. I was on airplane instead of boat.

ROSE: You're four days early. I can't believe it!

LUSIA: Is truth. Believe, please.

ROSE: *(Laughing.)* Oh, I didn't really mean . . . It's just an expression. Forget it.
(Beginning to speak more rapidly.)
Now, I don't know exactly what to do. I didn't expect to see you for a few more days yet. I'm not ready. Papa's not here since we thought you were coming later. But you've got to come right away, no matter what.

LUSIA: I got no place else.

ROSE: Of course you don't. Can you tell me the address? The street. The number where you are.
(She finds a pen and paper in the night table.)

LUSIA: Four-two-five La-fay-ette Street.

ROSE: Now, it'll be a few minutes. It's late and getting a taxi may take a while, but I'll be there.
(Holding phone with her chin she tidies the bed.)
Papa won't, you understand. I can't call him. He won't answer the phone on Sabbath, *Shabbes*, you know. What a funny time for you to come. Of course, it doesn't make any difference to me . . . Oh, wait a minute! This is silly. I'll see you soon and we can talk then. A lot. Anyway, I don't know how *you* feel about it . . . about anything, except you were traveling on Friday night, but it was an emergency . . .

LUSIA: Friday same like Monday, like Thursday.

ROSE: Lusia. Lushke, right?

LUSIA: Mama used to call me.

ROSE: *(Obviously uncomfortable, she pauses.)* Listen, Lusia,
I'll be right there. Goodbye now.

LUSIA: Goodbye now.
(LUSIA vanishes as ROSE hangs up.)

ROSE: What am I supposed to do?
*(She takes an extra blanket and throws it on the living
room couch.)*
Thanks, Papa!
*(ROSE turns on the radio, which takes a while to warm
up and start playing. She is both tearful and angry,
talking intermittently. She comes and goes, dressing herself, bit by bit, in quite stylish clothes, paying nervous
attention to her appearance.)*
Thanks a lot, Papa. . . . Anything for you, Papa . . .
What am I gonna do with her? . . . It's not fair!
*(Almost ready to leave, ROSE faces the audience, brush-
ing her hair in an unseen Downstage mirror in the
bedroom. Suddenly she stops, looks at her "reflection"
for several seconds, then speaks to herself very softly.*
It could've been you, Rose.
*(She stares at herself for another moment, then slams
down the brush.)*
It's all your fault, Papa!
(Picking up her coat and purse.)
Why can't you leave me alone!
*(She takes a deep breath, rehearses a smile in the mir-
ror, takes the H.I.A.S. address and goes into the living
room. She makes the sofa look as if she had been
sleeping there. The radio is still playing when she leaves.
The lights dim. The sound of the radio continues for a
while, then fades out.)*

Less than an hour later. The radio fades again with a different tune. The lights brighten as ROSE *enters, followed by* LUSIA, *who is pale and thin, wearing out-of-date, hand-me-down clothing: a blouse, skirt, and shapeless cardigan sweater.* ROSE *holds* LUSIA's *worn suitcase.* LUSIA *carries an old black handbag and a child's stuffed clown doll.* ROSE's *discomfort and self-consciousness are well-covered by her all-American prettiness and cheeriness.* LUSIA *is cautious and reserved, aloof, at times confused. She speaks softly and with little expression, a sharp contrast to* ROSE's *effusiveness.*

ROSE: *(Beginning offstage; rapidly, running on, as she turns off the radio and shows* LUSIA *around.)* It's not very big, but it's mine, at least, and I can do with it what I want, you see, and it's so much better than when I was living with Papa at the Greenspans' in Brooklyn. I'm sure you've heard of them. It was only supposed to be temporary, but that turned out to be sixteen years and the minute I hit twenty-one I moved out. This is the dinette and the kitchen's in there.
*(*LUSIA *follows and stands at the doorway, looking into the kitchen.* ROSE *goes off into kitchen. Offstage.)*
All the appliances came with the apartment. The newest kind of everything. There's nothing to it anymore—cooking and cleaning and keeping it all nice. You'll get used to it. You know, everything you see here, anything you want, just take it. It's all yours, too. Are you hungry? I mean do you want a sandwich . . .
(Voice only a wisp.)
. . . or an apple, maybe? Or something to drink?
*(*LUSIA *turns, looks away from doorway as* ROSE *enters.)*
A glass of milk or some juice or tea? I'll bet you drink tea, don't you, in a glass, like Papa?

(LUSIA nods. ROSE offers fruit from the table, LUSIA shakes her head.)
But if you're not hungry, let me show you the rest. Now, I was saying about the Greenspans, they're really very nice people, very old-fashioned, like Papa, but different. I know they're cousins or something, but I never could get the story straight.
(Proudly.)
That's called a Picture Window Convector in that window . . you know, a heater. It keeps it warm in the winter. I think they're third or fourth cousins, whatever that means, or she is, anyway, and I'm sure they'll want to meet you, but we can worry about that later.
(ROSE and LUSIA are in the bedroom.)
This is your room.
(She finally puts down the suitcase for the last time, and waits for a reaction.)

LUSIA: Is nice.

ROSE: In here's the closet. And the bathroom. It goes right through to the front hall.
(She goes off. LUSIA catches a glimpse of herself in the mirror, is surprised by her appearance, turns away from it quickly. ROSE returns with a stack of towels.)
Here's some clean towels. This is the big one for a bath or shower and this one's a face towel and here's the washcloth. See, I got them monogrammed . . . Oh, I'm sorry, Lusia. I'm just so excited. I'll slow down, I promise.
(She does, for a while, trying to be aware of LUSIA's possible difficulty in understanding, but gradually she will start rushing nervously again.)
What I mean to say is I had my initials put on them, all matching. And I just had "R.W." put on so when I get married, all I have to do is add another initial.

LUSIA: *Mazel tov.*

ROSE: What?

LUSIA: For your *t'noyim*.

ROSE: *(Puzzled, repeats the word unsurely.) T'noyim?*

LUSIA: Your marriage coming.

ROSE: *(Laughs, too much.)* Oh, not now, Lusia. I just meant *whenever*.

LUSIA: You don't have *hartseniu?*

ROSE: *Hartseniu?* Oh, you mean sweetheart. Well, no. Not really. There are several people I'm seeing, I mean going out with, spending time with . . . on dates . . . but nobody special. Do you want me to help you unpack?
(Indicates doll as she opens the suitcase. At first taken aback by what she sees, she awkwardly removes a plain, worn robe and pajamas, laying them out on the bed.)
You can put that on the bed or on the chair over there. I used to have a doll I slept with for years, a kind of rabbit or something. Mrs. Greenspan got it for me. Papa never would. She was very sweet sometimes. I always call her *Tanta* Perla. Even now when I visit.
*(*LUSIA *puts the doll on a chair or dresser.)*

LUSIA: I save it over here. (ROSE *brings a wrapped package from the closet.)*

ROSE: Here. This is for you.

LUSIA: *(Holding the present as if it might explode, staring at it.)* Thank you.

ROSE: Well, open it up.
*(*ROSE *starts to help* LUSIA *undo the wrappings.* LUSIA, *still staring at the gift, brushes* ROSE's *hands away and continues opening it on her own. She takes out a beautiful and elegant nightgown.)*
I didn't know what you had.
(She is suddenly somber, embarrassed.)
What they gave you. I thought you might like it.

LUSIA: *Shayn.* Pretty. Too pretty.

ROSE: Oh, nothing can be too pretty!

LUSIA: I mean to say, how much pretty.

ROSE: *So* pretty, then. "So," not "too."

LUSIA: So pretty. To sleep with. I cannot believe. So pretty.

ROSE: I'm glad you like it. Now, why don't you go wash up, I mean bathe, and I'll fix something to eat. I'll bet you're hungry, really. And you wear the nightgown. There's a real nice robe in the closet you can use to go with it. I have extras, honestly. And while I'm making lunch—I know it's the middle of the night, but it feels like lunch to me—you can freshen up and wash away all your traveling. You've come so far, in such a short time. I know you're tired, but we need to fatten you up a bit and get the roses back in your cheeks.

LUSIA: *(Refolding the nightgown.) Di roizn oif di bekelech* . . .

ROSE: I guess it's something like that. What are you doing? (LUSIA *has put the nightgown back in its box and is rewrapping it.)* Don't you like it?

LUSIA: Thank you. *(She takes the box and puts it next to the doll.)* I save it here.

ROSE: *(Urgently).* Oh, Lusia, wear it! Wear something pretty. You deserve something pretty, *(Picks up pajamas.)* not these awful things. *(Her voice is breaking.)* It's all so terrible! . . . You don't have . . . (LUSIA *looks away from* ROSE, *pretending interest in something else.)* There's nothing! . . . I don't know what . . .

(All at once, she stops, then continues speaking smoothly, in control.)
What I mean is you deserve something pretty. Like you. You could be so pretty.

LUSIA: *(An attempt at lightness.)* A shayna maidel? No.

ROSE: A pretty girl. That's right. That's who you are.

LUSIA: Mama used to say about you. "Ah, Rayzel . . ."
(She sighs, imitating MAMA. *Voice.)*
"a shayna maideleh."
(ROSE turns away rapidly. LUSIA *watches her for a moment, then pats the box.)*
I save it here.
(LUSIA picks up the stack of towels, fingering the monogram first, then the robe and pajamas, and goes into the living room. She turns back to ROSE, who is following her.)
Where you sleep?

ROSE: *(A forced cheerfulness, as before.)* Me? Oh, I sleep over here on the sofa. So I can keep that as a guest room. You know, in case someone comes for a visit or wants to stay over. Sometimes I think Papa might not want to take the subway all the way back to Brooklyn at night. Or *Tanta* Perla, when she visits. Really, I like to curl up out here. It means less to clean up and you know with me working there's hardly time to take care of things right. That's your room. Really it is and I sleep here all the time. Now, wait just one minute more.
(ROSE disappears into the bathroom. LUSIA *looks around slowly, as if catching her breath. She reaches out and almost touches the furniture.* ROSE *returns in a flurry.)*
I started the bath for you, so no more dillydallying. It smells wonderful. I put some bubble bath in it . . . "Night of Surrender" . . . can you imagine?
(ROSE is pushing LUSIA *toward the bathroom.* LUSIA *understands little of what's being said, but acquiesces, puzzled and a bit amazed.)*

It makes a whole lot of bubbles. It's absolutely sinful, really, it's so good!
(LUSIA *is now offstage. Shouting after* LUSIA.)
Stay in there a long time. As long as you like. We can sleep late tomorrow. There's nothing to do all day!
(ROSE *quickly starts setting the dinette table. Then she goes to the sofa, tidies the blanket. She suddenly stops, sits, grabs a sofa pillow and hugs it tightly, rocking slowly back and forth. Lights fade.*)

An hour or so later. As lights rise in the bedroom, wearing her faded robe, LUSIA *is fantasizing she is with her husband,* DUVID. *She calls him softly.* DUVID *appears, lights change to a fantasy glow.*

LUSIA: Duvid. Duvid . . . *Ich hob a sorpriz far dir.*

DUVID: *(Looking at* LUSIA.) *Vel ich es lib hobn?*
(LUSIA *does not look at* DUVID. *He remains behind her. She sees him only in her mind.)*

LUSIA: *Yo.*
(LUSIA *and* DUVID *now start speaking in unaccented English, setting the pattern for all the following scenes where the characters are assumed to be speaking Yiddish.)*
I *know* you'll like it.

DUVID: Let me see it.
(They are close together but not facing one another. DUVID *appears younger than* LUSIA, *filled with humor and energy, in his 20s, as* LUSIA *remembers him. She is wearing the gift nightgown hidden under her robe, although her package remains undisturbed.)*

LUSIA: First I want to tell you about my sister Rayzel. She doesn't feel like my sister. She's nervous with me. A stranger.

DUVID: Tell me why, Lushke.

LUSIA: It's because . . . *I'm* the stranger. I've invaded her house, but what can I do?

DUVID: Be yourself.

LUSIA: But Rayzel is afraid of me. She tries to hide it, avoids looking at me as one avoids a cripple. Or she does the opposite, stares at me and forgets to speak, like she's looking into a deep mirror. Then I'm scared.

DUVID: You're safe now.

LUSIA: *(Turning to look at him.)* Not until I find you.

DUVID: Can I see the surprise already?

LUSIA: All right, Duvidl. Turn around.
(He turns away. She takes off her robe.)
Now look.

DUVID: *(Turning to her, smiling.)* It's beautiful. You're beautiful. But so expensive! Can we afford it?

LUSIA: Rayzel gave it to me. A present. She gave it to me with innocence. With a longing, it seemed to me. But I didn't know how to thank her. I thought, "It's really a present for Duvid." It makes me feel closer to finding you . . . having something waiting for you. To give you. Like the clown for our baby. That was from Hanna. I told you already.

DUVID: *(Quietly.)* It's a handsome clown.

LUSIA: For a handsome child.

DUVID: A beautiful child.

LUSIA: Yours and mine.

DUVID: From you and me and your parents and mine and theirs, all the way back to Adam and Eve. A very important baby.

LUSIA: One of the most.
(Pause.)
Duvidl, lie down here, beside me.
(LUSIA reclines, DUVID follows.)
I want to tell you what I miss, here in my sister's bed in New York City. I miss it more than all the love and happiness between us.

DUVID: All right, Lushke. Tell me.

LUSIA: When we're asleep, with you all around me, like a warm shell, and I'm the egg safe inside, then I feel your dreams. Sometimes your foot twitches, sometimes a small sigh touches the back of my neck and I know you're running away or calling in your dream place. It's the most private place there is, the most secret, and you let me be there with you. This is what I miss most, Duvid . . . feeling your dreams. Even in a bed we've never shared, I miss going with you to your dreams.

DUVID: Man and wife are one life.

LUSIA: *(Sleepy.)* So many beds. And no beds.
(DUVID gets up, lowering LUSIA's head to the pillow.)

DUVID: *Gai schlofn, aiele.*
(Light begins to fade slowly.)

LUSIA: *(Giggling.) Mir kenen machn a kugel.*

DUVID: *(Tucking her in.) Gai schlofn, maideleh.*
(DUVID disappears in the fading light.)

LUSIA: *(Her voice fading, too.) Ich schlof . . . ich schlof . . .*
(Silence in the darkness. Both sisters are asleep. Slight movements come from LUSIA's bed. Gradually, her activity increases. She breaks the silence intermittently, whispering at first, then crying out.)
No. No! Mama. Mama? *Sprinze! Sprinzele!*
(LUSIA's voice grows louder and she is more active in her sleep. A dim light on ROSE in the living room. She sits up on the sofa and listens, not sure what awakened her.)
Loz mir oich gain! Ich vil oich, gain! Nein! Siz avek! Nein!
(ROSE gets up, moves toward the bedroom, uncertain whether or not to wake LUSIA. There are stronger sounds, moans, deep anguished cries from LUSIA.)
Vu . . . ? Ich ken zai mer nit zen! Ma—maaaa!
(ROSE turns on the radio and tries to listen to the music

so as not to hear LUSIA. *As* LUSIA's *nightmare contin-*
ues, ROSE *twice turns up the radio in order to drown it*
out.)
Avek! Aibik an aibik! Got! Mama! Mayn maideleh!
Sprinze!
*(*LUSIA's *words are almost impossible to distinguish,*
more of a continuous wail. With the radio at full vol-
ume ROSE *sits with her hands over her ears, trying to*
hide from LUSIA's *nightmare. Light fades to black. The*
radio continues to blare briefly, through the climax of
the music.)

The following day. Saturday, mid-morning ROSE *is heard softly humming a popular song. The morning light slowly comes up on her. She is wearing a robe and slippers, but looks dressed up. She is setting the table, trying to be quiet so as not to wake* LUSIA, *although* LUSIA *is not in sight and her bed is made.* ROSE *enjoys arranging the small feast. The doorbell rings, startling her. She goes to the front door.*

ROSE: Lusia!
(ROSE *follows* LUSIA *as she puts down her handbag.* LUSIA *is wearing the same clothes as when she arrived.*)
I thought you were still sleeping. I've been tiptoeing around. What were you doing? Where could you go?

LUSIA: To place I come to first. Where you come to get me.

ROSE: Whatever for? Did you forget something? I'm surprised they're even open today. You went all by yourself?

LUSIA: *(Struggling with language.)* I go read list. In books they got. And new names every day. People they find yet from the camps. Some coming yet from out woods where they been hiding.

ROSE: I know. I know, Lusia. But surely by now—

LUSIA: New names every day. And so I make *mine* list. You see? And sometimes maybe I find a person some place alive, some family, some friend. And this how I find Duvid, or he finding me, too.

ROSE: But that would take a miracle.

LUSIA: Is no miracle. Duvid is a . . . a *mensch*. Is only knowing Duvid is alive.

22

ROSE: *(Covering her discomfort.)* I see. Come, you'll tell me more. We'll eat.
(ROSE proudly leads LUSIA to the laden dinette table. LUSIA shrinks back, overwhelmed.)

LUSIA: Too much food! *So* much. No, *too* much, I think.

ROSE: You must eat, Lusia. You've got to eat enough. And there's plenty, really.
(Piling food on LUSIA's plate.)
I know you're the big sister, but you've got to let me take care of you, for now. Then, when everything's normal again, you'll be the big sister.
(ROSE pours a glass of milk. LUSIA sips at it, picks at the food. As they continue talking, they remain contrasted in manner. LUSIA is still, ROSE animated, using her hands a lot.)

LUSIA: Funny, big sister, baby sister. I have baby sister one time, long time . . .

ROSE: Ago.

LUSIA: Long time ago. So beautiful I think, and I take for walk in . . .

ROSE: Carriage?

LUSIA: Carriage, yes. I take for walk and show to friends mine baby *shvester*. Make me feel good. Happy. Then gone. And many years no sister but picture from America and letter from Papa and lady who takes care of.

ROSE: Mrs. Greenspan. *Tanta* Perla.

LUSIA: Yes. And then no more letter. No more sister.
(Voice.)
And carriage stays empty for too much years . . . And baby *shvester* woman now who want to take care *me*.

ROSE: I don't remember at all. I wish I did.

LUSIA: You don't remember even Mama?
(ROSE shakes her head.)
Nothing?

ROSE: I was only four when we left. It's so strange that
you have memories of me, that I was part of your life.
That I was born in another world. I don't remember
any of it. Just a feeling, maybe. Sometimes there's a
particular smell when something's cooking or a song
comes on the radio and all of a sudden I feel different,
like I'm in another place.

LUSIA: How you feel then?

ROSE: Warm. Safe. Sad.

LUSIA: Mama, that is. The feeling from Mama.
*(ROSE and LUSIA look at one another silently across
the table, each mirror to the other for a moment.)*

ROSE: Eat some more, Lusia. You're not eating enough.
(Pause while LUSIA picks at food.)
Lusia, have you wondered about it, thought why you
got sick and not me?

LUSIA: Mama says was plan from God. But she keeps
hold our passage, our tickets, till could not read no
more. Till thin like old leaf. Till long time after no
good, no one . . they no *loz* no one . . no one . . .
(She is frustrated, trying to find the English word.)

ROSE: Allowed.

LUSIA: Allowed leave Poland no more.

ROSE: And I was playing stickball and going to the movies
and eating Mello-Rolls!

LUSIA: What means this?

ROSE: Oh, it doesn't matter.
(She pushes away from the table, gets up.)
He should have gotten you out!

LUSIA: Mama told how whole America changes mind, wants no new Jewish, no new people no more. All fast like this
(Snaps her fingers.)
something happens no one got money. From streets with gold to nothing. And everyone, not just mine father.

ROSE: That was the Depression. It kept you away, but it didn't make any difference in my life. I remember having bad dreams when I was little, but I don't know what about. Everything else stayed the same; the food, the stories on the radio and *Tanta* Perla, like a bird chirping around me trying to give comfort after the bad dreams. But she never could.

LUSIA: *De varemsteh bet iz de mamas. Farshtaist?*

ROSE: Yeah, but how could I tell? Mama wasn't real to me. They'd never say her name, or yours. They called you "Them," talking in whispers or in certain looks so I could just pick up little bits of what was going on. And when I was older and could have understood, I knew it was forbidden. Papa wouldn't talk. Not about you, not about Mama. He would just say he was working it out or, later, that Roosevelt would take care of everyone over there. I tried to make myself a family out of the photographs and letters, but they were in Yiddish and I only learned to read English. *Tanta* Perla used to read them to me and translate. Papa never would. Then, when there were no more letters, I began to forget completely. By the time the war came, it was as if there had been no one there at all . . . until Papa found you. I still don't know exactly how to feel. I mean, I've had it pretty easy and you—

LUSIA: Mine father don't know I'm here yet?

ROSE: He'll be in *shul* all day. We can call him tonight or even go out there.

LUSIA: No. Tues-day I suppose to come on boat.

ROSE: Papa was going to come with me to meet you. He'll be mad if we don't let him know you're here.

LUSIA: This I remember good about Papa. He gets so mad. He makes a big voice, everybody is . . . *(She shakes.)*

ROSE: Nervous.

LUSIA: Nervous.

ROSE: In that way, he hasn't changed.

LUSIA: I remember him. Papa was a man very . . . pretty?

ROSE: Handsome? Papa?

LUSIA: Handsome. And I know from pictures, too. But everything must be certain way or he is so mad. And very . . .
(She gestures.)

ROSE: Strict.

LUSIA: Strict. But very proud when we all dress up. You, too. And Mama. Family all go out together. I see his face and I'm thinking how happy he is, how proud. He don't say nothing, but I can see. You know this face?

ROSE: I've never seen that look.
(Pause.)
We'll have to call him tomorrow.

LUSIA: We wait for Tuesday. Same as plan. Mine father is mine . . . *(She holds out her arm.)*
Like you and me?

ROSE: Flesh and blood.

LUSIA: Mine father is mine flesh and blood. On Tuesday, even, he will be mine flesh and blood. Now I got time to look some more for Duvid.

ROSE: But Lusia—

LUSIA: I look for Duvid so mine father could meet mine husband.

ROSE: *(Beginning to clear some of the food onto a tray.)* Can't you rest a little while? Let me take you around. You might get lost. It's such a big city.
(She picks up LUSIA's *milk.)*
Here. I'm going to fix this so you'll drink it. With chocolate.

LUSIA: *(Rising to stop* ROSE.*)* Big world, we find us each other, no? Here yet better. Listen.
*(*ROSE *sits.)*
I think big world hates Jewish. Today I go to office. I want to go, but don't know go this way or this.

ROSE: Left or right.

LUSIA: Don't know left or right. Everyone says in America police is good, will tell how to go. So, there's a police with a . . . suit like army . . .

ROSE: A uniform.

LUSIA: The police with uniform sits high up on horse on street talking to children. I think must be safe. I try talking, to make the words right, but was too feared . . .

ROSE: Frightened.

LUSIA: I want to say, "How you get to this place," but instead it comes out Yiddish. *"Vu iz di gaz?"* and I show card with office on. He looks at card and looks at me and goes over, like this, so he touches mine arm here. I think it's better I run away. Then he says something. You know what he says?
(Clears her throat, imitates policeman.)
Me nemt dem bos oif di gaze, an aroisgayn oif—

ROSE: *(Amazed.)* In Yiddish? He gave you directions in Yiddish! I'll bet you almost fainted! *Me . . . nemt . . . dem . . . bos . . .*

(LUSIA joins in with ROSE, *starting over.)*

LUSIA and ROSE: *Me nemt dem bos oif di gaz . . .*
        (ROSE starts laughing. She exits to the kitchen with the milk and tray.)

LUSIA: *(Sitting down, amazed.)* America!
        (The laughter continues.)

SCENE SEVEN

The action continues from the previous scene but now, in LUSIA*'s memory, it is Chernov, Poland, 1932. The lighting gradually begins to change to a soft glow as* ROSE*'s laughter is picked up offstage by* LUSIA*'s childhood friend* HANNA. HANNA *enters conspiratorially from the kitchen, bringing a piece of honey cake for herself and for* LUSIA. MAMA, LUSIA*'s mother, enters behind her.* HANNA *is about 14 years old in this scene, pretty, blonde, and lively.* MAMA *is in her mid-30s. They are dressed as they would be in a small town in Poland in 1932.* LUSIA *and* HANNA *are the same age, but* LUSIA*, as always in her memory scenes, appears as she is in the present. As* MAMA *enters, the girls are laughing and hiding their stolen cake. There is an easy physical affection between them.*

MAMA: *Fun tsu fil essen vert men crank* than from *under-*eating.
  *(*LUSIA *and* HANNA *giggle some more.)*

LUSIA: *Ober,* Mama, *s'iz* not a famine.

MAMA: *Gai farshtai a maidel!* Crying all night because some boy calls her a dumpling and now she can't stop eating.
  (She shows she is aware of the stolen cake.)
  Far be it from me to starve my own flesh and blood.

HANNA: Or me.

MAMA: What's the difference. You might as well be sisters.
  (She suddenly stiffens, listens.)
  Oy! The soup is boiling over!
  (She runs into the kitchen. From time to time we hear her singing offstage.)

29

HANNA: I love your mother. *(LUSIA nods.)* Only I wish she wasn't so sad. Even when she's joking, like now, I can see she's sad underneath.

LUSIA: *(Shrugging.)* She misses my sister. And Papa, I think. But mostly my sister.

HANNA: It seems like such a long time to be missing anyone.

LUSIA: Four years is nothing, Mama says. A child is a part of your body you never stop missing. Sometimes she goes like this . . .
(Quick intake of breath, hand to solar plexus.)
and she says, "Rayzel is sick, I can feel it," or "Rayzel is frightened. She's crying for her mama." It's the same as when someone's foot gets cut off and it still itches.

HANNA: What about you? Do you still miss them?

LUSIA: Rayzel, maybe. A little bit. I used to very much. I missed her and I was even jealous. Rayzel and Papa going to America and I was sick with scarlet fever. My hair all fell out. I looked terrible. I always thought we'd be going soon, too, and we still might, any day now, but then I'd miss you and I know you better than my sister.
(They lean across table, close together, holding hands.)
She's just a baby, anyway. Eight years old. So everything is good the way it is.

HANNA: *(An admission.)* I'm glad you got scarlet fever.

LUSIA: I'll tell you a secret, Hanna . . . Me, too.
(Looks toward kitchen before she goes on.)
You must swear never to tell this to anyone, ever . . .
(HANNA nods. They take an apparently oft-used swearing position.)
I'm glad I have Mama all to myself! When I was little and scared in the night she wouldn't let me in, with Papa there and the baby crying. But then, when they

left, she would open the covers like a great wing and pull me close to her. She's different without Papa here. She sings. And she never made jokes when he was around. I don't remember her laughing out loud. Papa used to make us be quiet. He would get angry all of a sudden and you never knew when.
(HANNA *and* LUSIA *continue glancing toward the kitchen through the following dialogue.*)

HANNA: Do you suppose she loves him?

LUSIA: I don't know. It's hard to think of your mother that way. I think she does, from far away. Maybe more, from far away. You know, my father's a whole lot older than she is.

HANNA: He is?

LUSIA: Around fifty-something.

HANNA: I think that's very romantic.

LUSIA: I don't.

HANNA: To have someone like that to take care of you, who knows more than you do. With silver-gray in his hair. My parents aren't romantic at all.

LUSIA: Your parents are just short. They don't look romantic, that's all. It's not their fault.

HANNA: But they never talk, except about business, and they sleep in two different beds.

LUSIA: They do?
(HANNA *nods.*)
Mine used to have one. I thought everyone's parents did.

HANNA: I will.

LUSIA: Me, too.

HANNA: With Duvid Pechenik?

LUSIA: Shhh!

HANNA: He called you "dumpling."

LUSIA: That means he likes me.

HANNA: But he's just your age.

LUSIA: A year older!

HANNA: He has pimples.

LUSIA: So do you.

HANNA: Stop it!
    (The girls' voices are getting louder. They stand up.)

LUSIA: You stop it!

HANNA: Dumpling!

LUSIA: Midget parents!

MAMA: *(Calling from offstage.)* What's going on in there?

LUSIA and HANNA: Nothing.

MAMA: *(Enters from the kitchen.)* You know, one old friend is worth ten new ones.

LUSIA: I know, Mama, but if she just wasn't so picky.

MAMA: If your grandma had a beard, she'd be your grandpa.

HANNA: We understand.
    (LUSIA and HANNA smile, giggle, and shake their heads.)

MAMA: *Kum mit mir, Hannele.* This time I'll *give* you *dem kuchen!*
    (LUSIA and HANNA look at each other, laughing, holding hands, as MAMA exits. HANNA kisses LUSIA on the cheek and runs after MAMA, giggling. ROSE, continuing her laughter at the policeman story, comes from the kitchen with the chocolate milk she promised LUSIA at

the end of the previous scene. The lighting returns to normal as she speaks.)

ROSE: *(Smiling.)* Here. See how you like it this way.
(LUSIA *looks at* ROSE, *surprised, as the lights fade to black.)*

Tuesday afternoon. A 1940s song is heard on the radio in the blackout. The lights come up in the bedroom and in the living room, where ROSE *is pacing and calling to* LUSIA *who is in the bedroom.*

ROSE: Hurry up and let me see!

LUSIA: *(Offstage.)* Not right. Is mistake!

ROSE: Well at least let me see!
(ROSE *sits on the sofa. As she waits impatiently,* LUSIA *is coming into the bedroom very slowly, facing directly toward the audience and looking at herself in the unseen mirror. She is uncomfortable, wearing a modish dress and shoes, which fit well but look out of place on her. She wobbles on the shoes.)*

LUSIA: You stay in living room. I come in there. Don't laugh. Is big mistake. Should be wearing this, Ginger Rogers.
(LUSIA *comes unsteadily into the living room.* ROSE *jumps up, pleased.)*

ROSE: Well, call up Fred Astaire! You look great! Turn around. It's perfect. Very American. All we need to do is fix your hair and you'll look like you were born here.

LUSIA: Was born in Poland, like you.

ROSE: *(Turning off the radio.)* But, don't you want to look like you belong, Lusia?

LUSIA: *(Her hand on her chest.)* When feeling here I am home, then I look like belonging more. Before war I have pretty dresses Mama made. I get some again

34

when I can buy myself. No more from you. Everything you want to give me. Already such a present and your bed, even, I sleep in. Yesterday before . . .

ROSE: The day before yesterday.

LUSIA: Yes. You bring me with to movie all day. Ginger Rogers. Cost a lot money. And food, food, food. All the time giving me to eat. And now clothes. No. Is too much. I get it myself.

ROSE: But you have nothing. Everything was taken.

LUSIA: You don't took it! I have suitcase, clothes from Red Cross. Same what everyone get. Soon one day, I go pick out new something. In store. And it has on it . . . what tell how much . . .

ROSE: A price tag.

LUSIA: A price tag on. No one wore it yet.
(ROSE looks at LUSIA quietly for awhile.)

ROSE: At least let me fix your hair, OK? Won't cost a penny. You won't know yourself.
(She sits LUSIA on a chair, begins fussing over her hair.)
I'm real good at this, I promise. Everyone at work thinks I get it done, but I always do mine myself. And I know you want to look your best for Papa. Now, don't worry, there's plenty of time. After he finishes at the store, he'll have a shave and maybe get his suit pressed, even though it doesn't need it, and get a shoeshine, too. Papa's always turned out like a gentleman. He's getting off early today to come and pick me up so we can meet you at the boat—but not yet. Sit still.

LUSIA: *(After a while.)* Rayzel, letters coming through front door say for Miss Rose White.

ROSE: I changed it, but not really. It's an exact translation.

LUSIA: Why?

ROSE: Just to sound like everyone once. For instance, you could change your name to Lucy.

LUSIA: What your father thinks to change his name, Weiss to White?

ROSE: His isn't changed. I've never told him I use the other. He probably wouldn't like it.

LUSIA: To change the name don't make you safe, anyway.

ROSE: *(Cheerfully brittle.)* What do you mean?

LUSIA: Someone knows Rose White is Rayzel Weiss, no matter. A new name don't make no difference.

ROSE: But that's not why—

LUSIA: They come take you when they want.

ROSE: It's just easier this way. I don't have to spell it for people.

LUSIA: Even you should wear a cross around neck, they know who you are. Always with Jewish, they find out the truth.

ROSE: *(Shaky, making an effort at being light.)* The truth is . . . your hair is all finished. Come and see.
(ROSE *and* LUSIA *go to the bedroom "mirror."* ROSE *stands back as* LUSIA *looks at her herself with an expression of surprise, pleasure, and bewilderment.)*

LUSIA: If I go in street like this—

ROSE: A very attractive young woman.

LUSIA: If Duvid walk near to me, he wouldn't know who I am!

ROSE: But you would know him.

LUSIA: Maybe he different, too. Thin or hair falls out maybe. Or hurt and walks different.

ROSE: But certainly before the war—

LUSIA: Before they take Duvid, already things was bad.
Hungry all the time, sickness, everyone frightened.
And this was six years ago. I am still a girl your age in
little place, no big city. No Ginger Rogers yet. Already
I look too much different only from time. I want
Duvid should know me, or a friend of him he shows a
picture, maybe.

ROSE: I see.

LUSIA: Thank you for pretty dress and shoes and for try
to make me look pretty, too. After I find—
(Doorbell, followed by an impatient knock on the door.)

ROSE: Papa!
*(LUSIA looks about, panicked, runs off into bathroom.
ROSE stares after her. The bell and knocking continue.)*
Just a minute, Papa. I'm coming.
(She goes to front door.)
Hello, Papa.
*(MORDECHAI follows ROSE into the living room, gives
her his hat and scarf. She puts them down while they
speak. She is trying to be natural, but is wary and
nervous.)*
You came early.

MORDECHAI: Greenspan closed up early.

ROSE: Was it crowded? The subway, I mean.

MORDECHAI: What do you think? Like always.

ROSE: It's getting warmer outside?

MORDECHAI: Warmer, colder. With spring in New York,
who can tell? When does she get in?

ROSE: Sit, Papa.
(MORDECHAI sits on the sofa, formally.)
You want some schnapps?
(She moves toward the kitchen.)

MORDECHAI: A half only. With a piece rye bread if you
    got it.

ROSE: *(Calling from offstage.)* Coming right up!

MORDECHAI: So, when does she get in?
    *(ROSE returns from kitchen with a shot glass half filled,
    a plate with two pieces of bread on it, and a napkin.
    She puts it on the table in front of MORDECHAI.)*

ROSE: Here you are, Papa. You want something else?
    *(MORDECHAI picks up one of the pieces of bread, puts
    it on the napkin, and gives it to ROSE.)*

MORDECHAI: You don't understand English? One piece
    only, I said.
    (Calls after her as she takes bread to kitchen.) Is a sin to
    waste even one piece bread and give me extra when in
    Europe they don't get nothing!
    *(MORDECHAI murmurs a brief prayer over the food,
    dips a corner of the piece of bread into the schnapps,
    then alternately sips and eats in a deliberate manner.
    ROSE returns with the napkin. She smiles, prepares.)*

ROSE: Papa, try not to be upset by this—

MORDECHAI: *(Interrupts his sipping/eating pattern.)* Some-
    thing's the matter?

ROSE: No. Everything's fine. Really good. It's good news
    about Lusia.
    (MORDECHAI looks at ROSE, waits. Trying to be cheerful.)
    Papa . . . She's here already.

MORDECHAI: *(Looking around him.)* Here? In this
    house?

ROSE: Yes. She came already.

MORDECHAI: When? Today earlier?

ROSE: *(Uncomfortable.)* Before.

MORDECHAI: *(Demanding.)* So where is she?

ROSE: She's getting dressed. She's a little nervous about seeing you.

MORDECHAI: Nervous from her father?

ROSE: She's been through a lot, Papa. All alone. And she's been waiting for such a long time—

MORDECHAI: What? I didn't try with everything what's in my power to get them out?

ROSE: That's not what I—

MORDECHAI: From a father she shouldn't be nervous.
(He rises.)
How long she's been in New York? Why you didn't tell me?

ROSE: I'll go and get her. Maybe she doesn't know you're here.
(ROSE hurries into the bedroom. MORDECHAI checks his appearance, sits, finishes the schnapps, and wipes his mouth delicately. He assumes a distinguished waiting pose. Calling softly.)
Lusia . . . It's Papa. He's waiting. Lusia!
(LUSIA, dressed in her own clothes again, comes into the bedroom, walks as if pre-set toward the living room, stops.)

LUSIA: Please, Rayzel, you come with me.

ROSE: I think it's better if you go alone.
(LUSIA sits on the foot of the bed, looking straight ahead, unmoving. ROSE, standing between the two rooms, looks from LUSIA to MORDECHAI and back again. The two of them are waiting stubbornly, in the same position. ROSE is trapped.)
Oh, all right. I'll come with you.
(LUSIA stands, walks ahead of ROSE, who follows at a distance, waits behind her. LUSIA enters the living room where MORDECHAI sits motionless, looking straight ahead, waiting.)

LUSIA: *Tateh?*

MORDECHAI: *(Looks at* LUSIA, *rises. He does not know her.)* Mine *tuchter*, Lusia Weiss?

LUSIA: *(Nods.)* Pechenik.

MORDECHAI: *(Moving toward* LUSIA *a little, still unsure of her identity.)* Lusia Weiss Pechenik *fun Chernov. Poyln?* (LUSIA *nods. They are at arm's length now.* ROSE *is watching unobtrusively.* MORDECHAI *takes* LUSIA *by the shoulders as if to embrace her. She is passive, unsure of her response. He keeps her at arm's length, then turns her around studying her.)*
You look different. You was only so . . . up to here, when I seen you the last time.

LUSIA: *Du oich zaist ois andersh.*

MORDECHAI: *Red nisht kein* Yiddish. Here we should speak American always. You, like your sister Rayzel. You become real American. Your *taten*, he does pretty good, but no so much as children. It took too long to get you over here, but you still can learn. You're young yet.
(Pause.)
You look a lot like my sister, Berta.

LUSIA: Everyone says this.

MORDECHAI: You know your Aunt Berta?

LUSIA: I . . . knew . . . her.

MORDECHAI: Sit.
(LUSIA sits carefully, apart from MORDECHAI, *who joins her on the sofa. As if reproaching* ROSE.)*
Maybe you should come with me to live at Greenspans'. You wouldn't get the right food here. *Tanta* Perla will fatten you up, even with her bad foot.

LUSIA: I stay with Rayzel. Until soon when I'll have mine own home. With Duvid.

MORDECHAI: And where is this Duvid?

LUSIA: Looking for me.

MORDECHAI: He knows your family is here?

LUSIA: He knows Weiss, Mordechai, and Rayzel. Maybe
he knows Greenspan in Brooklyn, too. I tell him such
long time ago. But Duvid is so smart, we find each
other. Until then, I stay with Rayzel.

MORDECHAI: And your sister . . . what does she think of
the arrangement?

ROSE: *(Joining* MORDECHAI *and* LUSIA.) It's good like this,
Papa. And I've got two weeks with no work . . .

MORDECHAI: You are not *shvesters.*
(Silent, shocked reaction.)
I mean to say, you ain't nothing alike.
(To ROSE.)
You take after . . . *fun* different sides the family.

LUSIA: Rayzel is like Mama.
(Pause.)

MORDECHAI: *(Abruptly, to* LUSIA.) Does she give you
enough to eat?
(To ROSE.)
Make sure it's the best. Kosher.
(Takes some bills out of his pocket and gives them to
ROSE. *To* LUSIA.)
Or does she make you sick with too much? From
overeating you suffer more than from undereating.
(After another pause, suddenly.)
Go get your coats. We're going.

ROSE and LUSIA: Where?

MORDECHAI: To eat in a restaurant. A big celebration.

ROSE: But I'm cooking dinner here, Papa. Pot roast.

MORDECHAI: Pot roast they got plenty at Fine and Schapiro.
Also, it's kosher.

ROSE: I fix kosher, Papa. You know that. For you always, special.
(MORDECHAI puts on his hat and scarf.)

MORDECHAI: I beg your pardon, *tuchter.* You can't make pot roast like Fine and Schapiro.
(MORDECHAI stands waiting near the front entrance-way. ROSE gets a coat, puts it on. LUSIA gets her handbag.)
What's the matter, she got no coat?

LUSIA: Is good like this. *Tsu hais.* Too hot outside.

MORDECHAI: *(To ROSE.)* Give her a coat. You got enough.

ROSE: I've tried, Papa. She won't.
(MORDECHAI hits floor with cane.)

MORDECHAI: Get the coat!
(ROSE leaves to get another coat. MORDECHAI considers for a moment, then decides to speak to LUSIA.)
You know, I got a big family in Poland. The Greenspans was the only ones here before me. Mine mama and *taten* was both dead before I leave Poland. I wrote down the others, all I could remember, so I don't forget.
(He is taking a notebook from a pocket.)
Some, I find out what happens from this organization or that or from Greenspan, maybe. Some I don't know yet.

LUSIA: I got list like you. The same.
(LUSIA takes out a similar notebook from her handbag. She and MORDECHAI move back into the living room. ROSE returns with the extra coat. She sees that something is going on and hesitates in the background, ready to leave. She will slowly be drawn into the reading of the lists, although she does not want to hear them. The reading has a ritualistic quality. MORDECHAI opens his notebook, studies it. LUSIA opens hers. She and MORDECHAI are on opposite sides of the room, both

facing Downstage. They read the lists slowly and qui-etly, as if checking an inventory. MORDECHAI *takes out a fountain pen and makes notations according to* LUSIA*'s information.)*

MORDECHAI: Artur and Salek Elias, nephews. Sons *fun* Berta Weiss Elias.

LUSIA: Artur Elias, dead. Murdered Maidanek concentration camp, nineteen and forty-two. Salek Elias, dead. Killed in battle, Warsaw, nineteen and forty-three, April.

MORDECHAI: Vladek Elias. Brother-in-law.

LUSIA: Vladek Elias. Murdered. Maidanek, nineteen and forty-two.

MORDECHAI: Berta Weiss Elias, sister.

LUSIA: Berta Weiss Elias. Murdered, Maidanek, nineteen and forty-two.

MORDECHAI: Zalmen Weiss, brother.

LUSIA: Zalmen Weiss, Esther Weiss, sons Motel and Ignacz Weiss, daughter Fela Weiss Friedman, grandchildren, Renia, Miriam, Moishe: murdered. All Auschwitz concentration camp, *fun* nineteen and forty-two until nineteen and forty-five.
*(*MORDECHAI *sits.* LUSIA *looks at him briefly, without expression, then continues reading.)*
Son-in-law, Benek Friedman, reported in Palestine, nineteen hundred and forty-six.

MORDECHAI: Markus Weiss, brother.

LUSIA: Markus Weiss. No word. Last was seen, Chernov, nineteen and forty-one.

MORDECHAI: Pesha Weiss, sister.

LUSIA: Pesha Weiss. Murdered, Auschwitz, nineteen and forty-three.

MORDECHAI: Karol and Janka Eisenman, mother-in-law and father-in-law.

LUSIA: Karol and Janka Eisenman. Murdered. Belzek. Nineteen and forty-two.

MORDECHAI: *(Softly.)* Your mother, may she rest in peace, I know what happened—

ROSE: *(An outburst.)* But I don't! Why won't you tell me how she died, Papa? Lusia?

MORDECHAI: It's enough to know she died in such a place.

ROSE: And all the others. So many! Names you never told me, Papa.
(She sits. She is cold, even with her coat on.)

MORDECHAI: They're dead.

LUSIA: *Ois geharget.* Murdered.
(Pause.)

MORDECHAI: And this they told me was no record. Shmuel Weiss and Minne Weiss, uncle and aunt.

LUSIA: Shmuel Weiss, no record. Minne Weiss, murdered, Chelmno, nineteen and forty-two.

MORDECHAI: Jakob Weiss and wife, cousins.

LUSIA: Jakob Weiss, murdered Treblinka, nineteen and forty-three. Maricia Weiss, murdered Birkenau, nineteen and forty-three. Daughters Gittel and Devorah Weiss, murdered, Birkenau, nineteen and forty-four.

MORDECHAI: *(Making a notation.)* For everything God does, there is a reason.
(He closes his book, puts it and pen in his pocket. He sits quietly, then notices that LUSIA is still standing with her list open.)
Noch mer?

LUSIA: Duvid Pechenik, husband to Lusia Weiss Pechenik, son-in-law to Mordechai Weiss, arrested, Chernov, Po-

land, nineteen hundred and forty. Sprinze Pechenik, daughter to Duvid Pechenik and Lusia Weiss Pechenik, *ainikl*—granddaugther—to Mordechai Weiss. Murdered. Auschwitz, nineteen hundred and forty-three.
(LUSIA *gently closes her book as lights fade to half.* MORDECHAI *and* ROSE *remain motionless during the following scene, which takes place in* LUSIA's *mind.*)
Al vos Got tut. He says there is a reason . . . Mama!
(MAMA, *her age the same as in the previous scene, enters, wiping her hands on her apron.* LUSIA *continues facing Downstage, looking at* MAMA, *seeing her only in her mind's eyes.*)

MAMA: *Es iz.*

LUSIA: There isn't! He says he knows, Mama. *Er vais!* He says he knows what happened to you. God's will.

MAMA: Your father never questions the will of God. And neither do I.

LUSIA: You're wrong! Even you, Mama!

MAMA: You don't play with God. I say it, your father always said it.

LUSIA: But he can't really know what happened. Why does he pretend to?

MAMA: Maybe he thinks he knows. And what difference does it make?

LUSIA: He's so sure. And safe.

MAMA: You want him to have some pain?

LUSIA: Yes!

MAMA: (*Laughing a little, looking at* MORDECHAI.) I remember when I felt the same way. But maybe, now, he's had enough already.

LUSIA: I don't care!

MAMA: You want to hurt an old man.

LUSIA: Yes! This one. Yes.

MAMA: Your own father?

LUSIA: He's not my father. He can't be. I don't know him. We're strangers. I don't know where I am. Where am I, Mama?

MAMA: With your family. Your flesh and blood. All that's left. My baby. My Rayzel, my pretty, little girl.
(She looks at MORDECHAI.*)*
And your father, he was my husband.

LUSIA: I'm sorry, Mama, but—

MAMA: Never be foolish and you'll never be sorry.

LUSIA: Mama, Mama, I'm in a dream! I don't want to touch them.

MAMA: *Sha!* They might hear you. *Sha, shtil, mayn kind.*

LUSIA: *(Weakly, as a helpless child.)* Mama! What should I do? What should I do? I don't know what to do! *Ich vais nit vos tsu ton!*
(Pause. MAMA *puts a finger to her lips. The moment passes. The lights fade to black.)*

*Later that evening. A loud blast of popular music on the
radio. The lights come up in the living room.* LUSIA *is seated
on the sofa, reading a magazine.* ROSE *is pacing.*

ROSE: *(Urgently.)* . . . But I want you to tell me! Please,
Lusia. How could you keep it from me? I have a right
to know!

LUSIA: I got a right to study, listen the music, the words,
so can talk more better. Get work, job.
(ROSE runs and turns off the radio.)

ROSE: That's not going to help you, Lusia. Talk with *me.*
I'll help you. That'll be much better. But, please,
you've got to tell me what happened.
(LUSIA gets up and moves away to bedroom. ROSE
follows.)

LUSIA: You seen that list, Rayzel. That's all it was. What
it says on that paper.
(LUSIA sits on bed, away from ROSE, *who continues to
pace.)*

ROSE: Lists. Lists! Your list, Papa's list. Like taking inventory of dry goods. Then, all through dinner, not a
word out of place. Not a tear. Not a sigh. Papa is
stone. But I'm not a baby and I want to know what
happened. I see pictures in the newspapers I can't
believe. And in the newsreels. I couldn't look, but I
wanted to see. Is that what it was really like? Was my
mother in one of those pictures? Were you? You're my
family, tell me!
(LUSIA looks at ROSE *before she speaks.)*

LUSIA: I cannot talk it. About it. Is all of living and dying.
Is too much from the . . . the *bainer* . . .

47

ROSE: *(Quietly.)* Bones.

LUSIA: The bones. The *hartz*. The *flaish*. I want not talk it
no more. OK?

ROSE: *(Sitting on the bed.)* Not even about Mama?

LUSIA: About Mama I tell you this . . . How was her *life*.
Almost happy, only except for missing you. She was
beautiful, skin like silk. Smooth and smells always
from clean, like soap. And saying all the time things
. . . words . . .

ROSE: Sayings.

LUSIA: Sayings to make things be better. She makes me
laugh, and Hanna, my friend, too. She sings, not too
good, like me. And cooks good, a lot, like you. She has
head in dreams, has dreams in head, forever. Things,
no matter how bad, be going better soon, says Mama.
And just like Papa, whatever happens is the will of
God.

ROSE: Even after—

LUSIA: Every day. The will of God. So that's Mama.
What I remember. This I can tell you.
(Pause, while ROSE *considers something.)*

ROSE: *(Softly.)* Can't you get it off?

LUSIA: What?

ROSE: The number. The number on your arm.

LUSIA: Is forever. Get it off? No.

ROSE: How did they do it, Lusia? Did it hurt? What did
you feel like when—

LUSIA: *(Going quickly into the living room.)* Now pardon,
please. I got to learn better English.

(ROSE exits through bathroom doorway, distraught. LUSIA *turns on radio. When it warms up, a voice is in the middle of a commercial. She begins repeating the words on the radio.* LUSIA *closes her eyes as the lights change to the fantasy glow.)*

In LUSIA's *memory, it is Chernov, Poland, 1939. The radio commercial changes to a lively Yiddish song.*

DUVID: *(Offstage, calling lightly.)* Lusia.
(DUVID *enters.* LUSIA *runs to him and they begin dancing all over the stage. They are laughing.)*

LUSIA: *Cher oif! Ich ken nitotemen!* Enough, Duvid!

DUVID: *(Whirling* LUSIA *even harder.) Shvahinker!* Weakling! Can't keep up?

LUSIA: *(Stopping, falling on sofa, out of breath.)* It's no use! You're right. I give up! You win, Duvid! You're in much better shape than I am!

DUVID: Condition, yes, I agree. Shape? Yours is better. It's my lungs. I'm running more now. They put Jews into a separate school, they help me build my strength. Twice a day now at twice the distance as before. And no more cigarettes. I take advantage of the rationing to improve my health.

LUSIA: A real opportunist.

DUVID: That's me.

LUSIA: You call too much attention to yourself with all this running. You could get to work five minutes later. Mr. Grubman understands about school. You're too noticeable. You stand out.

DUVID: It doesn't matter. No one can catch up with me.

LUSIA: No?
LUSIA *lunges for* DUVID, *beginning a game of tag as frenetic as the dancing. It's unclear who is chasing whom.*

Finally, DUVID *has* LUSIA *cornered. He advances menacingly. She screams, laughing.)*
No, Duvid, no! Mama will come in! What will she think?

DUVID: We're almost married. She'll encourage me.

LUSIA: No! Mama! Mama! Help! *(*DUVID *grabs* LUSIA *and kisses her. Their embrace is innocent and chaste, somewhat awkward.)*
I don't know if I can be married and still live here. With you and Mama. It seems indecent.

DUVID: She's used to me. She likes me. I like her. She used to give me cookies, cakes, handouts—all the time when I was a kid. So now I get you. Another handout. No difference.
*(*LUSIA *squeals and strikes out at* DUVID. *He grabs her again.)*

LUSIA: But Duvidl . . . In my room. And Mama right next door. It's not right. I won't be able to—

DUVID: To what?

LUSIA: *(Pushes* DUVID *away, then goes after him.)* I must be marrying you for your money since you have no brains.

DUVID: I'm marrying you for your mother's gefilte fish! You'd better watch out or I won't take you to America.

LUSIA: And Mama.

DUVID: And Mama. I won't take her either.

LUSIA: Anyway, between the Germans and the Russians, we're stuck.

DUVID: Leave it to me.
(Posing.)
With brains, brawn, and money, I'll lead the way.

LUSIA: *(Suddenly serious.)* You mean it, don't you.

DUVID: Of course I mean it. Together we can do anything. You'll see. Man and wife.

LUSIA: Man and wife.
(As the scene shifts from LUSIA's *memory to her fantasy of the future, they begin to dance romantically to a 1940s song playing in the background.)*
Just like the old days.

DUVID: It hurts to think back.

LUSIA: We won't then.
(Pause. They are barely moving.)
Duvid.

DUVID: Yes?

LUSIA: Nothing. I like to say your name.

DUVID: Lusia.
*(*LUSIA *and* DUVID *stop dancing. Their embrace becomes more intense.)*

LUSIA: Wait, Duvid. My father. He'll be here any minute. And Rayzel. She's right in the bathroom there.

DUVID: So? We're married, you know.

LUSIA: I know, but still . . .

DUVID: But still?
(He laughs, teasing.)
Some things never change!
*(*DUVID *continues to move in on* LUSIA, *who is backing off.)*

LUSIA: *(Laughing.)* Stop it! Duvid! *Du gaist tsu shnel! Nein!* Papa! Rayzel!
(They are about to kiss again when ROSE *enters from the bathroom.)*

ROSE: Lusia!
*(*LUSIA *hears* ROSE, *the music cuts off, radio comes back, and the lighting returns to normal. The sisters*

look at each other while DUVID *recedes.* LUSIA *is out of breath.* ROSE *is puzzled and alarmed.)*
What is it, Lusia? What are you doing? What happened?

LUSIA: *(Also surprised.)* Rayzel? Oh, *mine shvester* . . .
(Looking about, bewildered, struggling with the language.)
I just am sitting here. Then I am remembering . . .
something . . .
(Smiling gently, hopeful.)
that is gonna happen.

END OF ACT ONE

Act II

SCENE ONE

Midday, the following Sunday. In the blackout, a regular thumping sound is heard. MORDECHAI *counting with each thump. As the lights rise slowly,* MORDECHAI *is jumping back and forth over his cane, which is lying on the living room floor. He is encouraging* LUSIA *to count with him.* LUSIA, *looking less pale than in Act I, gets confused, is mostly silent. As the scene begins, the counting has reached "94."* ROSE *enters from the kitchen to straighten chairs in the dinette and finish cleaning up after a meal. She is wearing a dish towel/apron. When she sees the scene in the living room, she stops, astonished.*

MORDECHAI: Ninety-five, ninety-six, ninety-seven, ninety-eight—

ROSE: Papa!

MORDECHAI: *(Waving* ROSE *off, not losing a beat.)* Sha! Ninety-nine, one hundred! *(*MORDECHAI *stops, breathes deeply, as if taking a bow, talks to* LUSIA, *who only nods in response.)*
Look. You see? I'm breathing like a teenager. In two months I'll be seventy. Also is teaching you how to count American.
(To ROSE.*)*
I want she should know what a strong family she comes from.
*(*MORDECHAI *turns back to* LUSIA, *while* ROSE *finishes tidying the dinette.)*

55

Mine grandfather lived to a hundred two, still walking every day with a milk-wagon three miles. And he never missed in his life even one Sabbath in the *shul*. Finally, he died *fun* a frostbite that turned green. As it happened, he got frozen in the snow, with the milk coming up *fun* the cans, on Monday. He died just in time before sunset Friday and that's the first one he missed. This story I heard *fun* mine own mother, may she rest in peace, many times as a boy. So you know you're *fun* strong people.
(To ROSE.)
You, too. Both of you. Even when I was born, on that same night, came soldiers on horses, cossacks, making trouble, setting fires. But I didn't cry and call attention. I didn't make even a peep.

ROSE: *(Coming over and sitting.)* Papa, you told me this before, didn't you? When I was little. I never heard you tell a story since then.

MORDECHAI: So now you heard.

ROSE: *(Enthusiastically.)* Tell another, Papa. From when you were a boy, about your family. We'd both like to hear it. Lusia?
(LUSIA *nods.)*

MORDECHAI: *(Abruptly, to* ROSE.) Stories should only mean something. They should teach something, like Torah. If it's not teaching something, it's a waste of time to talk so much! I want she should know also how much respect this family got.
(To LUSIA.)
When I first come here, I started as a stock boy, doing errands, no English. Now, Greenspan's an old man. Only seventy-two, but already an old man and I'm running the place. He, Greenspan, he calls me Morty, but no one else. Customers, salesgirls, everyone, "Good morning, Mr. Weiss" and "Let me speak to Mr. Weiss, he knows the answer." Look, I got even a business

card. You see that? Mordechai Weiss. You understand? It's important you should know this. No matter
how much you suffer, what you lose your family, you
don't hardly know no English, you still can be a person
with respect, which is worth more than all the tea in
China. You understand? Your sister, she got it easier.
American all the way. Nobody's gonna give her no
trouble. You see that?

ROSE: Papa, I've had to work hard, too, and—

MORDECHAI: You got brains and health, that's what you're
supposed to do! So don't tell me.

ROSE: I know it's not the same, but I never had anyone to
help me with—

MORDECHAI: *(Hitting the floor with his cane.) Tuchter!
Mit* God's *hilf*, you got brains and health you help
yourself! This way you can live through anything.
(To LUSIA.)
All right, *tuchter*. Get your hat and coat. We're going.
(He puts on his hat and stands up, ready to leave.)

ROSE: Where, Papa? Lusia and I are planning to—

MORDECHAI: She comes with me to Brooklyn to meet
Greenspan, to see the place I been living all these
years! What would be her home if things work out and
there's no Depression.

ROSE: Well, OK. I guess I should visit *Tanta* Perla, anyway.

MORDECHAI: No. I want she should come by herself. All
of this, Brooklyn, Greenspan, you already know. Now
it's her turn.

LUSIA: Papa, I want Rayzel should come.

MORDECHAI: Rayzel is staying here. She's got to do her
tax.

LUSIA: I got to help her.
(Sits.)

MORDECHAI: *(To* ROSE.*)* Tell your sister.

ROSE: He's right, Lusia. You go ahead. There's nothing you can help with. I've got things to do, business, from my job. I'll be better off by myself. And you'll get to see what might have been your home.

MORDECHAI: So go get your hat and coat.
*(*MORDECHAI *waits in front hall while* LUSIA *goes into bedroom. She returns carrying her pocketbook, no hat or coat.)*
This is it again? No coat?
(To ROSE.*)*
Get your sister a coat.
*(*ROSE *moves to do so,* LUSIA *stops her.)*

LUSIA: *(Looking hard at* MORDECHAI.*)* I'm going with you like you want. I don't wear no coat.
*(*MORDECHAI, *taken aback, looks from* LUSIA *to* ROSE *and back, then waves* LUSIA *on ahead of him. To* ROSE.*)*
Is a good day Sunday to be home, no?
*(*ROSE *forces a smile and nods.* LUSIA *exits.* MORDECHAI *starts to leave behind her.)*

ROSE: Bye, Papa.

MORDECHAI: *(Turning back.)* You made a good meal, Rayzel.
(He turns to leave again, stops.)
The fish was a little bit salty, but the eggs was good.
(He continues out.)

ROSE: *(As he exits.)* Thanks, Papa. Bye.

MORDECHAI: *Zei gezunt.*
*(*ROSE *goes into the dinette as if to clean some more, removes the dish towel from her waist, throws the towel onto the table, and goes into the living room, turns on the radio, picks up a magazine, and tries to read. When the music comes on she waits a moment, listening, then turns it off. She tries to read again, finds herself staring*

*at the page, not seeing the words. She closes the maga-
zine, puts it down and, hesitantly, goes into the bedroom. She picks up the doll, looks at it, puts it down,
and starts to leave. She changes her mind and touches*
LUSIA's *robe, which is on the foot of the bed. She
slowly puts it on, looking in the mirror. Suddenly she
hears something. It is the sound of a child crying softly.
Frightened, she looks around.)*

ROSE: Who is it? Who's here?
(The child's voice occasionally calls "Mama." ROSE
*speaks softly, unable to identify the source of the voice.
She turns in the room.)*
What's the matter? . . . How did you get in here? . . .
Don't be afraid . . . Where are you?
(The sound has grown louder.)
Who are you?
(ROSE *catches herself in the "mirror" opposite the foot
of the bed, turns toward the audience to see herself. At
this moment, the weeping stops. She realizes that she is
alone as she stares at her image in the mirror. She
touches her dry eyes. Lights fade.)*

SCENE TWO

Tuesday afternoon. When lights rise, LUSIA *is in the living room, energetically cleaning with a brush and cloth. She is humming, on her knees. The lights shift to a glow. Facing Downstage, she smiles as* HANNA *enters behind her.*

LUSIA: Hanna.

HANNA: *Ken ich arayn kumen?*

LUSIA: *(Running to embrace her.)* Hanna! *Ch'ob gevart far dir!*
(HANNA now looks LUSIA*'s age and is dressed in outdated, secondhand clothes likes hers.)*

HANNA: But your sister isn't home. Are you sure it's all right?

LUSIA: *(Leading* HANNA *by the hand. When she speaks, it is reminiscent of the first time* ROSE *showed her the apartment.)* If she were here, she'd invite you in herself. You have to see everything. It's even got things we didn't know to dream about! Look here, look at this: carpet like a cloud. You could sleep on the floor. And what about this? This is a machine that makes it warm, like the middle of July, on the coldest winter day!
(HANNA exclaims over everything.)
And, Hanna, wait till you see the kitchen!

HANNA: Does it have a stove? A real one?

LUSIA: It runs on electricity, that's what you won't believe.
(LUSIA runs into the kitchen.)

HANNA: *(Looking after her.)* No!

LUSIA: *(Offstage.)* Yes! I mean it! And there's a machine

that washes your clothes and then the dishes. Oh, it leaves a little egg sometimes, that you have to do over. But mostly it's like having a housemaid—five maids—to do the work.
(LUSIA *comes back into the dinette.*)
And you put your garbage outside the back door and while you sleep, a man comes on an elevator and takes it away.

HANNA: There's something left to throw away?

LUSIA: Too much. You can't eat enough to use it up before it spoils.

HANNA: We used to dream of a piece of bread . . .
(She rubs the table top.)
Everything is so clean!

LUSIA: *(Back in the living room, turns to HANNA.)* Wait until you see the bathroom! Everything white and shiny. A bathtub big enough to swim in and water hot enough to boil an egg if you wanted to.

HANNA: Inside the house?
(LUSIA *nods. They laugh.*)
And I can stay here?

LUSIA: Of course. Rose is out of town on business. You can have the bedroom—I'll show it to you in a minute— and I'll sleep here. It's where I'm used to.
(She poses on the sofa like ROSE. *They look at each other, then* LUSIA *sits up and speaks softly.)*
You know that whatever is mine is yours, Hanna.

HANNA: *(Arms held out to* LUSIA, *who joins her.)* Whatever is mine is yours.

LUSIA: A half a potato.

HANNA: A quarter of a potato . . . A cup of barley-water soup.

LUSIA: A spoonful of soup. Half is yours.

HANNA: More than half sometimes.

LUSIA: Whoever needs it more.

HANNA: Whoever wants it less.
(*Pause. The lights are beginning a slow change to cold blue.*)

LUSIA: You kept me alive.

HANNA: Your life was something to live for.

LUSIA: You were all I had left.

HANNA: You were everything.
(*Pause. Their bodies are beginning to change, distort. They are clutching, rather than holding each other.*)

LUSIA: If you had no one you were dead . . .

HANNA: . . . much faster. If you had someone . . .

LUSIA: . . . you had to live so they would live.
(*It is cold. A distant wind is blowing.* HANNA *and* LUSIA *reach around each other even further, leaning on one another for physical support and warmth.* HANNA *breaks away, looks around.*)

HANNA: (*Whispering.*) Now follow me. Into the house.
(HANNA *moves toward the bedroom.* LUSIA *pulls back, frightened.*)

LUSIA: But we can't go in there.
(*Both women are weak and cold.* HANNA *has the energy given by a fever.*)

HANNA: Yes we can!

LUSIA: No!

HANNA: But we're free!

LUSIA: I don't believe it.

HANNA: Liberated.

LUSIA: Liberated.

HANNA: He said it was all right. The Russian on his horse. He said the whole town belongs to us now.

LUSIA: *(Close to* HANNA, *outside the bedroom, whispering, terrified.)* But there might be someone in there.

HANNA: So what? Old women and babies only. They were left behind.

LUSIA: I wouldn't put my foot in a German house.

HANNA: It was a Polish house before they took it.

LUSIA: It's no good, Hanna. It had Nazis in it.

HANNA: We're free. We can go where we want to. We can take anything. Food. Clothes. Take back what they stole. He told us. The Russian on his horse. In Yiddish. Who would have guessed? In Yiddish.

LUSIA: But there's a grandmother in there, Hanna. And a little baby. We might frighten them.

HANNA: How can you say such a thing? Your mother wasn't frightened?
(As HANNA *speaks,* LUSIA *covers her ears, humming, to drown her out.)*
Sprinze wasn't frightened on the way to the ovens? They took your sweet little girl. They took your mother. They took everything from us, but we can't take a warm coat or a piece of sausage from—

LUSIA: Stop! I don't want to hear! We can't be like them! We can't do what they did! And I don't want a warm coat. I want to be cold like the dead ones. I don't want—

HANNA: Shhh! See. She ran away.
(Leading LUSIA *into the bedroom. The wind stops.)*
Took the baby out the window. Look. Lusia. It's empty. Come. There's nobody here. Look. A bowl of cereal. For the baby. Oatmeal. Still hot. And a sausage. Milk.

LUSIA: It will make you sick to eat all at once. Just take a little bit, Hanna!
(But HANNA is eating the imaginary food rapidly, insanely. Then she sees the doll. She picks it up and cradles it like a baby.)

HANNA: This is for my baby.

LUSIA: It belongs to another child.

HANNA: It's for the future. For my baby.

LUSIA: You'd bring a child into this world? Anyway, we can't have children anymore.

HANNA: I can.

LUSIA: You can't, Hanna. I can't. We stopped our periods. We're not women anymore. We don't have women's bodies.

HANNA: We will.
(LUSIA turns away from her.)
Eat. And get round. Soft. Clean. Bleed.
(She is weakening, having difficulty breathing, crumples on the bed. LUSIA turns to her.)
Have babies. You and Duvid.

LUSIA: *(Moving to comfort HANNA.)* All right, Hanna. We'll have babies.

HANNA: *(Hugging the doll tightly.)* And me . . .

LUSIA: You with someone wonderful like Duvid.

HANNA: A handsome Russian soldier.

LUSIA: On a horse.

HANNA: Who, out of nowhere, speaks Yiddish.

LUSIA: *(Laughing.)* The horse?

HANNA: Even the horse speaks Yiddish.
(HANNA and LUSIA both start laughing wildly until HANNA begins to cough. She weakens greatly.)

LUSIA: Shh. Soon you'll be better. Now there'll be doctors and medicine.

HANNA: *(Giving* LUSIA *the doll.)* I ate too much. You were right. But it's a good reason to be sick for a change. Overeating. What would mama say?
(She rises with effort.)
Here, you take the doll.

LUSIA: But it's yours.

HANNA: You'll need it before I do. Don't even know the Russian's name yet. Let go of me.
(She pushes LUSIA *away.)*
Hold the doll. Protect it. I'm going to throw up and I don't want to get it dirty.
*(*LUSIA *stands up as* HANNA *exits.)*
Not dirty. Go away from me, Lusia. *Gai avek fun mir. Avek!*
*(*LUSIA *is standing alone, hugging the doll, as the lights return to normal. She looks at the doll, caresses it.)*

LUSIA: Hannele! Who can I laugh with now?
*(*LUSIA *quickly puts the doll down. She runs back to her cleaning, furiously. She sneezes.)*

She sneezes again. ROSE *enters from bathroom through bedroom with cleanser and rags on her way to kitchen.*

ROSE: I wish you'd stop, Lusia, and take it easy. It doesn't need to be *that* clean.

LUSIA: I like to.

ROSE: I've never heard of anyone cleaning that way. I'm sure no one's ever done it in here before.

LUSIA: That's how come I . . . achoom?

ROSE: *(As she disappears into kitchen.)* Sneeze.

LUSIA: Sneeze. First time I use that word. Sneeze. For something to be too much clean is impossible. Anyway, if I live here, I do something to help.

ROSE: *(Coming into living room with dusting cloth.)* But you could stop for a while and rest. If you will, I will, OK? You could get in the bathtub and soak all day. Go on. I know how you love that bubble bath. Sometimes I think you'll never come out.

LUSIA: I'm sorry. I'll try to be more faster.

ROSE: That's not what I meant. You can stay in as long as you like. Only I don't think you should always be working. Half the day at the immigrant office and here the rest of the time. You won't even come to the movies anymore. You deserve some peace. Outside of the bath.

LUSIA: *(A bit huffy.)* Peace I'll get when this all cleaned up. OK?
*(*ROSE *shrugs, goes back to her dusting and polishing*

with added energy. LUSIA *and* ROSE *are both working furiously. Each begins singing to herself,* ROSE *a popular song,* LUSIA *a song in Yiddish, softly, not really aware that she is singing. It is the same song she hummed earlier to drown out* HANNA. ROSE, *however, is aware of* LUSIA's *song and listens to it as she continues her work. Then she is still, just watching her sister.)*

ROSE: That's pretty.
*(*LUSIA *stops singing, keeps working.)*
No, don't stop. That sounded so nice. It reminds me of something. Lusia, it's one of those times I told you about. Did my—our—mother used to sing that song?

LUSIA: That song, no. But sing, yes, always when she's working in the house or cooking or sewing something. But not too good, same like me. Maybe this is what reminds you.

ROSE: No, you have a sweet voice. Sing some more. Teach me. I'd like to learn it.
(Pause.)

LUSIA: This song is from the camps.

ROSE: *(Quickly.)* Oh, I'm sorry.
(She turns away.)

LUSIA: *(Watching* ROSE.*)* Rayzel. Rose. It don't matter. Is a good song. Happy. About how the world will be after war is over. Was a song then about future, yes? So now is a song about now. I teach you it. Come.
*(*ROSE *sits beside* LUSIA *on the floor.* LUSIA *sings, as a teacher.)*
O, di velt vet verren shayna,
libe greser, sine klayna
You know what this means?

ROSE: Some of it. Not every word.

LUSIA: It says the world will be beautiful. Love will get more and hate . . .
(She gestures.)

ROSE: Less.

LUSIA: Less. And that's for everybody. Between women and between men and between one country and the other country.
(LUSIA *begins the song again.* ROSE *joins in tentatively for the first two lines. When the verse is repeated she joins in again, singing more strongly.)*

LUSIA and ROSE: *(Singing.)*
O, di velt vet verren shayna,
libe greser, sine klayna
tvishn froyen, tvishn mener,
tvishn land un land.

O, di velt vet verren shayna,
(LUSIA *is singing more strongly, forgetting* ROSE.)

libe greser, sine klayna
tvishn froyen, tvishn mener,
(ROSE, *watching* LUSIA, *fades out and* LUSIA *finishes alone.)*

tvishn land un land.
(Pause.)

LUSIA: Enough for now. Is a longer song. Too much. Enough. Hanna used to sing with me.

ROSE: Is she a friend of yours?
(LUSIA *nods, returns to her energetic cleaning.)*
From the war?

LUSIA: And from before. From children together.

ROSE: *(Treading carefully.)* Was she liberated with you?
(LUSIA *nods.* ROSE *is relieved.)*
You came through it all together?

LUSIA: Is why I live now. And Duvid.

ROSE: Well, where is she? We could bring her here, you know. You don't only have to be a family to sponsor someone. If the two of you went through it together and came out of it together . . .

LUSIA: Hanna was too sick. Tee . . . ty-phus, you know. She was all . . . nothing left of her. I say when I really look for first time in hospital, "But Hanna, we is bones, both of us, nothing but bones. We never be womens again." She say old saying, like Mama. Too sick hardly to talk, she says, *"Bainer on flaish iz do; flaish on bainer iz nito!"*
(She laughs.)
Farshtaist?

ROSE: I think so.

LUSIA: "Bones without meat you can have; meat without bones, is impossible." This way she makes jokes and was living only one more day.
(ROSE turns away and goes off into kitchen.)
But she was free. And clean. And was thinking things for the future.
(LUSIA goes back to her brushing. ROSE returns shortly, with a full picnic basket.)

ROSE: I know I can't get you to leave that spot, so I brought a picnic.
(ROSE unwraps chicken legs, bread and cheese, etc. laying them on the cloth on the floor near LUSIA.)

LUSIA: For this I can stop.

ROSE: Your appetite is improving.

LUSIA: Mine sister is a good cook. An expert.
(LUSIA and ROSE eat heartily. ROSE takes chocolate milk from basket and gives it to LUSIA.)

ROSE: With chocolate?

LUSIA: With chocolate.
(Enjoys drinking some.)

This chocolate in the milk you learn from your *Tanta* Perla, no?

ROSE: She used to do anything to get me to drink milk. Because she thought she should.

LUSIA: She seems like kind woman when I meet her. Like bird, like you say, but with hurt foot, hop . . . ?
(ROSE nods.)
. . . hopping to get seeds, to get warm.

ROSE: Worm.

LUSIA: Worm. Warm. Worm.
(She considers.)
To get a worm to sing little bird song about bird troubles.

ROSE: You know her perfectly! That's just what she's like. More a sparrow than a hen. *Tanta* Perla could not hatch an egg.

LUSIA: In my house, your house, too, in Chernov, before the war, for long time we got chickens. Many. Eggs every day and some extra makes for more chickens for soup Mama makes delicious. In Brooklyn I see no one get chickens and much . . . hard where you walk, how you say this?

ROSE: Pavement. Sidewalks.

LUSIA: Much pavement sidewalks not good for to grow trees with fruit. We have in the summer baby apples.

ROSE: Crab apples.

LUSIA: And *barnes* . . . pears. Mama can make grow anything and then make for bread jelly, jam, all good, for whole year.

ROSE: That's something I never tasted homemade.

LUSIA: This we have even when trouble begins because is right by house. Until all Jewish got to move to one place. But before—how you say—married . . . still childrens, me and Duvid, only fifteen, sixteen, we take—steal—from Mama the jam and bread and have . . . like this . . .

ROSE: A picnic.

LUSIA: By the river in woods. We feel so bad, like thief, so have to eat up all this jam, the whole bottle, with a spoon—

ROSE: To hide the evidence!

LUSIA: And is best pic-nic I ever have.
(Pause.)
Rayzel, yesterday in the morning a man came into immigrant office. Is very thin, much more than me. And teeth black and poor clothes, much worser than mine. He has list, he says, lots of names what happened last six years Poland, even from beginning of war, like time when Duvid been arrested. He kept list secret in camps and copied very neat, many pages, who died, who lived, who escaped, how, where. Of course, this I want to see right away. The man say no, will no give list to nobody. Only will sell. For money.

ROSE: How awful!

LUSIA: No. He needs money for food, clothes, to live. This list is his work, his talent. He's not a bad man.

ROSE: Well, what happened? What did you do?

LUSIA: I can do nothing. I send him to a man more important. Today I'll see what happens. I think maybe Duvid is on this list.

ROSE: What makes you think so?

LUSIA: Is time for Duvid. Is already—
(The doorbell rings. Again. Then pounding on the door. ROSE *jumps up in panic.)*

ROSE: It's Papa! What's he doing here now? In the middle
    of the day!
    (She calls.)
    Papa?
    *(ROSE is answered by more pounding. Tossing the cheese
    to LUSIA.)*
    The cheese. Hide the cheese! I'm supposed to keep
    kosher . . . Coming, Papa!
    *(LUSIA starts to run off with the cheese as the pound-
    ing continues. She runs back: very serious.)*

LUSIA: But, Rayzel, is a sin to lie to a papa, no?
    (ROSE freezes, stares helplessly at LUSIA. Suddenly.)

ROSE: Di milch!
    *(ROSE and LUSIA are both frantic, grabbing the milk
    and other offending items. At the same time, they are
    beginning to laugh very hard. When LUSIA is safely in
    the kitchen, and the remnants of the picnic are looking
    kosher on the floor, ROSE goes to open the door.
    MORDECHAI enters behind her, wearing a hat but no
    scarf. It's a warm spring day. He carries a shoebox tied
    with a string.)*

MORDECHAI: It's nice. I got nothing better to do all day
    than to knock on a door.
    *(LUSIA returns from kitchen. Both she and ROSE are
    working to control their laughter. Seeing the picnic.)*
    What goes on here?

ROSE: A . . . picnic, Papa.

LUSIA: Rayzel just cleaned up the table so we been eating
    on the floor.

MORDECHAI: So, if I sweep the floor, maybe you'll eat on
    the table!
    *(This is too much. ROSE and LUSIA burst out laughing,
    holding onto each other to keep from falling. MORDECHAI
    is amazed at the success of his joke.)*
    Is good *shvesters* should laugh together.

(ROSE and LUSIA recover, aware for a moment of their physical closeness.)

ROSE: I'm sorry, Papa. You want something? A drink, maybe? I've got some delicious chicken.

MORDECHAI: *(Putting down his hat and cane in the dinette.)* No, no. I got all I need. I want you two should clean up your picnic and come sit down. I'm on important business.
(During the next several lines of dialogue ROSE and LUSIA pick up and put away the picnic and cleaning things. MORDECHAI is arranging chairs around the dinette table.)

ROSE: How come you left the store? You really surprised us.

MORDECHAI: Today they're doing inventory. For this, I can leave. For this, Greenspan can manage alone. He can count. He can write down numbers in a book. Especially when I got something more important.

ROSE: Does it have to do with that box? A surprise, maybe?

MORDECHAI: That's it. Exactly.

ROSE: Lusia, you see what your being here has done? Everything's topsy-turvy. Surprises in the middle of the week, yet. Papa taking off early. Amazing!

MORDECHAI: Enough, already. Sit. Both.
(ROSE and LUSIA sit. MORDECHAI, still standing, holds the box.)
This box is the most important thing in the world. In the universe, even, for us. In here is your family, your history, who and where you're coming from. It's proof who you are.
(He puts the box on the table.)
It's proof of people we'll never see no more, parts of them alive still, in you. And better yet, in your chil-

dren, with God's help. Old pictures I had *fun* mine parents, *fun* aunts and uncles. Some I stopped showing you when you was little, Rayzel, always making you cry too much for your mother, may she rest in peace, or for Lushke, as you used to say.

ROSE: I don't remember that!

MORDECHAI: These I showed you again later when they were the same to you like pictures in your schoolbooks and they didn't make you cry no more.

ROSE: They were just faces. You *were*, Lusia, far away and different.

MORDECHAI: All these I got. I want Lusia and you should look at them together, remember together. Maybe like that it would mean more. All names and what year, what place, is written on the back. Anything you want to know you write down on a piece paper so you don't forget and next time I'll tell you what's what.

ROSE: We will, Papa.

MORDECHAI: Lusia?
(LUSIA *nods. Pause as* MORDECHAI *sits between his daughters. He includes* LUSIA, *but is primarily speaking to* ROSE, *presenting something to her.*)
Some months ago came to see me a Polish woman. Nobility. A countess, a friend *fun* your mother—an employer—who your mother made beautiful dresses by hand and she, your mother, would give this rich woman sometimes a present, baked goods or fruit from her garden.
(LUSIA *looks stricken, turns away.*)
This countess, of course, is not a Jew, but, still, a good woman. She came in person. She wouldn't take a chance to send something what it might get lost. In person, only, she wants to see me.

MAMA'S VOICE: *Ich blayb mit mayn kind . . .*
(LUSIA *pulls further away from the others.* MAMA *en-*

ters the bedroom area slowly, as MORDECHAI *speaks.
She is older, in her late 40s, moving around in the
outer edges of the space. She carries a knapsack. Her
head is covered by a scarf.)*

MORDECHAI: She never sat down, didn't take off her coat
or take a glass of tea. But she gave me a bundle *fun*
your mother.
(ROSE reaches for the box.)
Wait.
(MORDECHAI unties the package very slowly. ROSE's
*attention is on the package, too. Unheard by the oth-
ers,* LUSIA *suddenly gets up, comes forward, paces as
she talks to* MAMA, *apart from her.)*

LUSIA: Mama! *Farvos bistu nit gegangen?* I told you to go!

MAMA: It was impossible.

LUSIA: But you would be here now! You'd be here with
me and Rayzel and Papa. I told you to go! If only—

MAMA: If your grandma had a beard, she'd be your
grandpa . . .

LUSIA: Don't do that. It's not funny. Don't be so stubborn!

MORDECHAI: Come, Lusia, sit. Stop pacing. It makes me
so I can't think.
*(MAMA is signaling LUSIA to hush. LUSIA sits. MORDE-
CHAI has the package opened. He puts the box aside
and removes a smaller bundle wrapped in a head scarf
identical to the one MAMA is wearing. LUSIA is frozen
by it. The Voices begin quietly. Gently beginning to
open the bundle.)*
This is exactly how she gave it to me. I put it back the
same so you could see. She didn't touch it from the
way your mother first put it.
*(MAMA is sitting on the bed. In the dim, cold light, she
opens the knapsack and removes an old candlestick,
which she holds, barely moving.)*

It was many years since I heard anything from *mine*
wife. The first thing I found, in here, like this, was a
letter for me. It was from over three years before.
When I read it the worst already happened, but I
didn't know yet. The countess carried this around the
world until she came to America. Even if not Jewish,
they knew to run from Hitler. Anyway, this from your
mother she carried like a holy package, I couldn't
believe it. The next is some pictures you never seen of
your sister here when she graduated school and this is
a wedding . . .

(MORDECHAI *is passing the pictures to* ROSE, *intending
her to hand them on to* LUSIA. LUSIA *turns away, slowly
gets up.*)

ROSE: Papa, can't we look at these later? I think it's hard
for her. It's much too painful.

(LUSIA *is on her way to the bedroom. Voices fade.*)

MORDECHAI: *(Touching his head.)* All these pictures she's
got here inside, already. This paper don't make the
pain, believe me.

(ROSE *starts to follow* LUSIA. MORDECHAI *holds her
back. They continue to look quietly at photos while
the scene in the bedroom continues. The lighting emphasis changes.*)

LUSIA: Mama, you've got to go with her and get out of
this horrible place!

MAMA: *(Repacking knapsack.)* Don't argue.

LUSIA: But she wants to protect you, to take a chance
herself because she thinks so much of you.

MAMA: She's a wonderful woman.

LUSIA: Then go!

MAMA: All right. She said they have room for one more.
You. But not the baby. Not Sprinze. You want to
come, too?

LUSIA: How dare you! Don't be crazy, Mama!

MAMA: You stay with your child, I say with my child.

LUSIA: But this is different. I'm not helpless like the baby. You have another daughter, too. You could be with Rayzel again. Finally, Mama. And Papa.

MAMA: When you have a grandchild, you have two children. Here where I am, I have two. There, where I may never arrive, is one I lost long ago. I won't take the chance of losing more.

LUSIA: But, Mama, then you had no choice. This time you do.

MAMA: It only looks like a choice. If God wanted us to be in America, you never would have caught scarlet fever. Your father would not have had such business troubles—

LUSIA: I'll never agree with you, never! About God.

MAMA: God doesn't care if you agree or not. He does what He does. God doesn't argue and God doesn't change His mind. Besides, maybe where they're sending us this time will be an improvement. In the country somewhere. At least not a ghetto. Trees, maybe, some flowers—

LUSIA: Mama, listen. Please! Anything the Nazis do will only be worse, never better. You go with the countess. I'm young. I'll do all right. I have the medicine for Sprinze. It puts her to sleep for two days so she won't cry. I'll carry her in my knapsack. Others have done it. They won't even know I have a baby.

MAMA: I stay with my child.
(She kisses LUSIA on the forehead.)
. . . *Ich blayb mit mayn kind.*

ROSE: *(Standing and moving toward LUSIA as lights return to normal in dinette and fade in bedroom.)*

Lusia, look!
(LUSIA, *returning to reality, leaves the bedroom and meets* ROSE, *who is holding a small silver spoon with a sealed letter and scarf.* MAMA *exits.*)
Papa says this is my baby spoon! I used to eat with it.
(LUSIA *takes the spoon.*)

LUSIA: Sometimes I feed you with this.

ROSE: And a letter for me, from Mama!
(ROSE *is holding the letter out to* LUSIA. LUSIA *takes it, hands it back, with the spoon. She goes directly, angrily, to* MORDECHAI.*)

LUSIA: How long ago this countess visits?

MORDECHAI: November, December, maybe.

LUSIA: Mama sends these things for Rayzel. Why you don't give them before?

MORDECHAI: Until I knew for certain—

LUSIA: And now you already know for a long time!

MORDECHAI: I was hoping we should all be a family again—

LUSIA: *(Overlapping.)* Is no more hoping! Mama's dead! We was supposed to come here! Was your promise. I want Rayzel should know this.
(To ROSE.*)*
Mama was all ready we should wait. So we wait. Then comes a letter from your *Tanta* Perla. She's asking us why Papa won't take no money. Some group in Brooklyn is giving him money so we could come and he should pay it back later. But Papa says no. He won't take from no one.

MORDECHAI: This you should understand.
(Pounding the table.)
Not to owe nothing!
(He rises.)

ROSE: But, Papa!

MORDECHAI: What? I knew was coming the Depression?
I knew the doors would be closed here? I had a crystal
ball showed ten years ahead to Hitler?
(Pause.)
Every penny I made since went to bring them over
myself!
(ROSE is looking hard at MORDECHAI.)

LUSIA: Then it don't matter no more. Is too late.
(To MORDECHAI.)
And now you don't want even to read to her what
Mama is saying. Now you don't want even to touch
something of Mama's. From shame. From shame!

MORDECHAI: *(Calming, quietly.)* Rayzel, who you want
should read your Mama's letter, me or your sister? Say
only the truth.
(ROSE holds out the later to LUSIA.)
It should be better a woman. *Tanta* Perla, maybe.
*(ROSE holds the letter out again. LUSIA takes it, holding
it away from herself. She moves slowly into the living
room and sits down. MORDECHAI gets up, goes to get
his hat and cane.)*
Lusia, read the letter for your sister. I'll wait for you
downstairs. When you're finished, you come. I got
some new places we should leave word about your
husband.
*(MORDECHAI is almost out the door, remembers some-
thing. He comes back and removes a photograph from
his vest pocket, shows it to LUSIA and then ROSE. LUSIA
closes her eyes.)*

ROSE: A pretty girl.

MORDECHAI: Age sixteen only.

ROSE: It's Mama, isn't it?

MORDECHAI: *(He nods.)* A shayna maidel.

(MORDECHAI puts the photo back into his pocket and leaves.)

ROSE: *(After a moment, amazed, as she sits.)* He must keep that picture with him all the time.

LUSIA: *(Thrusting envelope out to ROSE.)* You open, please. Is your letter.
(ROSE opens the envelope carefully.)

ROSE: It's very fresh. Like it was just written.

LUSIA: Mama keeps the paper, I think, for long time before she sends this letter. Was all ready for when someone comes like countess. I never seen her write nothing.
(ROSE hands the open letter to LUSIA, who hesitates, then smells the scent of the letter. LUSIA can hardly speak.)
Is Mama. Before . . .
(She tries to give the letter back to ROSE.)
Ich ken nit . . . Ken nit!
(ROSE keeps looking at her, waiting. LUSIA breathes deeply, composes herself, then slowly sits apart from ROSE, begins shakily, relaxes more as she feels and enjoys her recognition of MAMA in the words. As she continues ROSE stiffens, reacting almost politely, as someone at a tea party. There are no tears.)
Mayn tyereh tuchter, Rayzel . . .
Mine dearest daughter, Rayzel,

   I'm not a learned woman. I wish I could be so I could say everything to you the right way. For a long time I have written and I know it could happen you don't get the letters. This one is meant by God's will to reach you. Maybe it is the last one for a time so I want to tell you everything how I feel.

   If I could really be with you and put around you mine arms, it would be much better, but that is impossible. It cannot be. If I cannot hold you in mine arms, I hold you anyway in mine heart and this is true for every day in your life since you was born, if you was in Chernov, Poland, or Brooklyn, New York, America.

I want you should have your baby spoon. Your favorite, just your size and you could first feed yourself with it. Every day since you and Papa went away, I keep it in a pocket with me, to touch what you touch. I knew I would give it back to you before you were five years old and now look what happened! Well, who are we to question the plan from God? Now when you have this baby spoon, you must get a feeling from your mother. Sometime you will have a child to use it, too, and she will feel from her grandmother. Or, who knows, maybe the family will be together by then.

You would think I would have more to tell you besides this baby spoon; advice and so forth, but I can't think of anything more important right now. You can't put life on a piece of paper. Or love. I am not a smart person with writing down words, but I wish you understand how I am feeling for you, mine pretty little girl.

Your only mother,
Liba Eisenman Weiss
Chernov, Poland, June four, nineteen hundred and forty-two.

(LUSIA *and* ROSE *sit silently for awhile, then* LUSIA *puts the letter back in the envelope, kisses it, and gives it to* ROSE.)

ROSE: Thank you, Lusia.
(*Silence again for a time, then* LUSIA *stands up.*)

LUSIA: Papa's waiting.
(ROSE *nods.* LUSIA *gets her pocketbook.* ROSE *gives her the scarf in which everything was wrapped.* LUSIA *leans over and kisses* ROSE *on the forehead.* LUSIA *exits.* ROSE *opens the letter again, tries to drink in the scent.* ROSE *clasps the letter and the spoon, which she is still holding*

to herself. She sounds at first like the child's voice she heard earlier.)

ROSE: Mama. Mama!
(Now the sound that comes from her is a chant, an intoning that is trying to make something happen. Each repetition becomes more intense, almost angry.)
Mamamamamamamamamama.
Mamamamamamamamamama.
Mamamamamamamamamama!
(The Voices are emerging out of ROSE's *call. She moves into the bedroom. She puts down the letter and spoon. The Voices are continuous. She gets the pen from the night table. Slowly and deliberately, as if she is carving, she draws a number on her left forearm and stares at it. The sound of the Voices is a comfort to her. As it becomes* MAMA's *lullaby, she sits on the bed, arms outstretched, welcoming it. She embraces the sound and herself, as the lights dim. Slowly, she curls up on the bed as the Voices fade.)*

Several hours later. Silence. The dim light continues. LUSIA
enters, excited, puts down her bag.

LUSIA: Rayzel? Rose?
(LUSIA *looks around; in the dinette, the kitchen doorway, then goes into the bedroom. Seeing* ROSE *turned
away, asleep,* LUSIA *begins to talk with excitement as
she turns on the bed lamp and sits on the bed.)*
Rayzel, you can't take no nap now! I got to tell you
something. Something good. Papa took me to place I
never been yet.
(ROSE *is slowly awakening. She is groggy, confused.)*
The woman there knows about Duvid. I can tell. She
don't say nothing, but—
(ROSE *begins to sit up.)*
—is a smile in her eyes when we talk and she says will
I be at home so she can call me on telephone if—
(As ROSE *moves,* LUSIA *suddenly sees the number on
her arm. She cries out.)*
Rayzel!
(She grabs ROSE's *arm, looks at the number, then at*
ROSE.)
What you done to yourself?
(LUSIA *drops the arm and pulls back, horrified, not
wanting to see.)*
What you done?
(She stands away from ROSE *who, as a bewildered
child, reaches out.)*

ROSE: Lushke.
(After a moment, LUSIA *rushes to the bed and takes*
ROSE *in her arms, cradling her, comforting her, strok-
ing her hair.)*

83

LUSIA: *Sha, shtil, mayn kind. Sha. Shtil.*
(*As* LUSIA *is gently rocking* ROSE, *Mama's scarf still on her head the phone rings. The sisters slowly pull apart, not letting go of each other.* LUSIA *is reaching for the phone as the lights fade to black.*)

An hour later. The radio is playing. Lights up in the living room. LUSIA *is alone, waiting, pacing, patting pillows, running to look in the mirror. With hands trembling, she turns off the radio, runs to the front door, returns at once, sits rigidly, waiting. There is a gentle knock on the door. She jumps, holds tightly to herself, remaining stiffly seated.*

DUVID: *(Offstage.)* Lusia? Lusia, *ken ich arayn kumen?*

LUSIA: *Kum arayn.* [Then close the door behind you. *(If no door closing sound available.)*]
*(*DUVID *enters, carrying a small suitcase. He is older, smaller, thinner than in* LUSIA*'s memory, dressed in an ill-fitting suit and hat. He, too, is frightened, unsure.* LUSIA *does not look at him.)*

DUVID: *S'ez ich,* Duvid.
(He stands back, puts down the case.)

LUSIA: Duvid.

DUVID: Can't you look at me?

LUSIA: No, I can't.

DUVID: Why not?

LUSIA: I'm afraid. It's too much. You're real. It can't be.

DUVID: Look. See.
*(*LUSIA *slowly stands, turns, and faces him.)*

LUSIA: So thin! So much older! Lines.
*(*DUVID *looks back at her silently.)*

DUVID: *(After a while.)* Can I take off my hat?
*(*DUVID *removes his hat.* LUSIA *takes it from him care-*

85

fully, like a bomb that might explode, puts it down fast. She scrutinizes him.)
You're the same.
(LUSIA shakes her head.)
The same.

LUSIA: A different person. A stranger.

DUVID: Lusia.

LUSIA: Six years.

DUVID: I knew where you were. Until the liberation. Then I lost you. But I knew you were alive.

LUSIA: I lost you from the beginning. Messages came, and word from people I didn't know, but they all said something different. So you disappeared. One said you died. Then I was sure you lived.

DUVID: I was in many places. I got moved.

LUSIA: Are you well?

DUVID: Getting stronger. You?

LUSIA: Healthy. Getting fat from my sister's cooking.
(Pause.)
There's too much! How to tell so much!

DUVID: I know everything. It was the same with me.
(He moves toward her.)
Lusia . . .

LUSIA: *(Turning away from him.)*
I can't.
(He moves again.)
I can't!
(They are frozen in this impasse. From a distance, then growing louder and closer, is the sound of gentle, joyful music. Gradually the lights shift in mood and the fantasy glow rises throughout the apartment. There is a sound of laughter and merriment, a party, also coming

closer. Mama, in a party dress, carries the old candle-
stick with a lighted candle in it, and a tray of honeycake.
She puts these on the dinette table. She looks behind
her.)

MAMA: *Kum shoin, Mordechai!*
(MORDECHAI, *wearing a flower in his lapel, enters with*
glasses of wine on a tray. ROSE *and* HANNA *are coming*
from the other side, laughing, admiring each other's
finery. All but ROSE *speak accented English.* MAMA
motions for LUSIA *to go to* DUVID.)
Give your husband a hug, Lushke, then we'll have
something to eat.
(LUSIA *looks at* DUVID, *then back at the festivities.*
MORDECHAI *puts his tray on the dinette table.)*

MORDECHAI: First, a toast. Everybody take a glass.
(They all take glasses; there is an undercurrent of
excitement.)
Let's say thanks to God for this happy occasion. With
his blessing, will come soon a baby. May it not be long
until the *bris.*
(Silence while they all drink, then another burst of
laughter. HANNA *whirls past* LUSIA, *who reaches for, but*
cannot touch her. HANNA *giggles as she evades the touch.)*

HANNA: Look at this dress, Lusia, how it catch the light.
Rayzel come with me to pick it out special for you and
Duvid.

ROSE: *(Turning slowly, to* LUSIA.) Tomorrow, if you want,
we'll all go get one for you. OK, Papa?

MAMA: Your father says yes.

MORDECHAI: Why not?
(ROSE *runs and hugs* MAMA. *Their embrace is slow and*
full, with a reach beyond reality. MORDECHAI *contin-*
ues after a while.)
Now, Liba, let go of Rayzel for a minute. I got something to show you.

(MORDECHAI *begins to dance.*)
Seventy years old and what condition, eh? A regular
Fred Astaire.
(*Invites* MAMA *to dance.*)
And here's my Ginger Rogers.
(*The music swells into the foreground of the scene.*
MORDECHAI *and* MAMA *dance together in an old-
fashioned way. The others enjoy.* MORDECHAI *becomes
the beginning of a chain, leading* MAMA *around* LUSIA
and DUVID. ROSE *and* HANNA *add on. They all circle
the couple smiling, with slow, slightly exaggerated movements. It is as if* LUSIA *and* DUVID *were the pivot of a
fantasy merry-go-round, the others circling in an attempt to pull them together. As the end of the chain
passes,* LUSIA *turns to* DUVID. *The others leave on tiptoe
so as not to disturb them.* HANNA *and* ROSE *look at*
LUSIA *and* DUVID *and giggle before they leave.* MAMA
and MORDECHAI *watch for a moment, his arm around
her shoulders. They kiss happily, then remove their
trays and steal away. As* MAMA *is almost offstage, she
and* LUSIA *turn to each other.* MAMA *again waves* LUSIA
closer to DUVID, *then she blows out the candle and is
gone. The music comes to an end and the lighting returns
to normal.* DUVID *and* LUSIA *are standing as they were
before the party began. They speak without accents again.*)

LUSIA: (*Dropping her "I can't" position.*) There's no one
left but us.

DUVID: I know.

LUSIA: (*Turning to him.*) Duvid.

DUVID: What?

LUSIA: Your name. Duvid.

DUVID: Lushke!
(LUSIA *and* DUVID *embrace, not moving, clinging to
each other. After a few moments, they lean back to
look at one another.*)

LUSIA: I see her in you. Sprinze. And you never saw her at all. She was beautiful.
(DUVID moves away.)
She looked like you . . .
(DUVID sits on the sofa heavily, looking away. LUSIA waits, then sits beside him. Trying to comfort.)
I was wrong, Duvid. There's more than you and me left.
(DUVID does not respond. After a while, LUSIA continues in another tone.)
Do you speak any English, Duvid?

DUVID: *A bissell. Farvos?*

LUSIA: *Mayn shvester Rayzel farshtait a bissel Yiddish, ober si red nor English.*
(Continues in accented English.)
A hundred percent American, she is. I want we should speak English for Rayzel.

DUVID: This I can do. Slow, maybe.

LUSIA: We practice a little, yes?
(DUVID nods. LUSIA continues with great pride, taking DUVID's hands and speaking slowly so he will understand.)
Duvid. Mine sister, when you call up on telephone, went in taxi, forget what time it is, all the way to Brooklyn where lives Papa. She's gonna bring him here personally, in person. *Farshtaist?*

DUVID: I understand.

LUSIA: So we sit here, wait.

DUVID: We got many yours . . . *years* yet for to talk.
(They both smile, almost laugh, when he gets through the sentence. A small echo of old days.)

LUSIA: So. In any minute now is coming a key in the door or they knock or ring the bell maybe. Then, Duvid—
(The doorbell rings. LUSIA carefully lets go of DUVID's hands, smiling. She goes to the door. DUVID rises and

waits. LUSIA *returns with* ROSE *and* MORDECHAI. *The sisters stand together, arms about each other.* MORDECHAI *remains apart, uncertain.)*

Duvid . . . I want you should meet . . . mine family.

*(*ROSE *and* LUSIA *are watching* MORDECHAI, *who has not moved. He and* DUVID *observe each other from* MORDECHAI'*s chosen distance.* ROSE *motions* MORDE-CHAI *to come closer. He does, looking at his daughters.* ROSE *nods, encouraging him.* MORDECHAI *moves slowly to* DUVID, *taking him by the shoulders as he did* LUSIA *when first seeing her. He hesitates for a moment, then slides his arms around* DUVID. *The men embrace fully. Without turning* MORDECHAI *lowers one arm and reaches out behind himself. Still holding tightly to* ROSE, LUSIA *steps forward and takes* MORDECHAI'*s hand. Slowly, the lights fade to black.)*

END OF PLAY

Mordechai—when in Yiddish mode, or by Lusia with gutteral "ch." In "American," as if Mordekai.

Lusia—as if *Lew*sha

Duvid—as if *Doo*vid (as in "good")

Pechenik—as if Peh-*cheh*-nik (ch as in "cow")

Chernov—as if *Chair*noff (ch as in "chew")

Glossary of Yiddish Words and Expressions
Not Translated Within Script

A shayna maidel translates literally as "a pretty girl." It describes inner beauty and is an expression of love and of yearning hope.

ACT—SCENE

I-1   *Hashem yish-mereynu mikhol ro veyishmor ses nafsheynu.*
May God protect us from all evil and may He protect our souls.

Shtetl/Village

Licht. Mir muzn hobn licht!
Light. We must have light!

I-2   *Ich hob im in drerd!*
He should rot in Hell! (Literally: I have him in dirt.)

Shvesters/Sisters

91

Ain flaish/One flesh

Tanta/Aunt

Gai schlofen/Go to sleep

I-4   *Mazel tov*/Good luck

T'noyim/Engagement

Hartseniu/Sweetheart

Di roizn oif di bekelech
The roses in the cheeks

I-5   *Ich hob a sorpriz far dir.*
I have a surprise for you.

Vel ich es lib hobn?/Will I like it?

Yo/Yes

Aiele/Egg

Mir kenen machn a kugel./We could make a
pudding.

Loz mir oich gain./Let me go, too.

Ich vil oich gain./I want to go, too.

Nein/No

S'iz avek/She's gone

Vu?/Where?

Ich ken zai mer nit zen./I can't see them any more.

Aibik un aibik/Forever and ever

Got/God

I-6   *Mensch*/A real man

Di varemsteh bet iz de mames. Farshtaist?
The warmest bed is the mama's. Understand?

Shul/Synagogue

Me nemt dem bos oif di gaz, un aroisgayn oif—
You take the bus here, and get off at—

I-7   *Fun tsu fil essen vert men crank—*
From overeating one gets sicker—

Ober/But

Gai farshtai a maidel!/Go understand a girl!

Kum mit mir/Come with me

Dem kuchn/The cake

I-8   *Tuchter*/Daughter

Du oich zaist ois andersh/You look different, too.

Taten/Father

Red nisht kein Yiddish./Don't speak Yiddish.

Noch mer?/Even more?

Als vos Got tut/All that God does

Es iz./There is.

Sha, shtil, mayn kind./Hush, still, my child.

Ich vais nit vos tsu ton!/I don't know what to do!

I-10   *Ich ken nit otemen!*/I can't breathe!

Du gaist tsu schnel./You're going too fast.

II-1   *Hilf*/Help

Zei gezunt/Goodbye (Literally: Go good)

II-2   *Ken ich arayn kumen?*/Can I come in?

Ch'ob gevart far dir./I was waiting for you.

Gai avek fun mir./Go away from me.

II-3   *Farvos bistu nit gegangen?*/Why didn't you go?

Ich ken nit./I cannot.

II-5   *S'ez ich*/It's I

Kum shoin/Come on already

bris/circumcision ceremony observed when a boy is eight days old.

bissel/little

ober si red nor English/but she only speaks English

PLUME   **MERIDIAN**

EXCEPTIONAL PLAYS

(0452)

☐ **A RAISIN IN THE SUN by Lorrain Hansberry.** From one of the most potent voices in the American theater comes A RAISIN IN THE SUN, which touched the taproots of black American life as never before and won the New York Critics Circle Award. This Twenty-Fifth Anniversary edition also includes Hansberry's last play, THE SIGN IN SIDNEY BRUSTEIN'S WINDOW, which became a theater legend. "Changed American theater forever!"—*New York Times*　　　(259428—$8.95)

☐ **BLACK DRAMA ANTHOLOGY Edited by Woodie King and Ron Milner.** Here are twenty-three extraordinary and powerful plays by writers who brought a dazzling new dimension to the American theater. Includes works by Imamu Amiri Baraka (LeRoi Jones), Archie Shepp, Douglas Turner Ward, Langston Hughes, Ed Bullins, Ron Zuber, and many others who gave voice to the anger, passion and pride that shaped a movement, and continue to energize the American theater today.
(009022—$6.95)

☐ **THE NORMAL HEART by Larry Kramer.** An explosive drama about our most terrifying and troubling medical crises today: the AIDS epidemic. It tells the story of very private lives caught up in the heartrending ordeal of suffering and doom—an ordeal that was largely ignored for reasons of politics and majority morality. "The most outspoken play around."—Frank Rich, *The New York Times*　　(257980—$6.95)

☐ **FENCES: A play by August Wilson.** The author of the 1984-85 Broadway season's best play, *Ma Rainey's Black Bottom,* returns with another powerful, stunning dramatic work. "Always absorbing . . . The work's protagonist—and great creation—is a Vesuvius of rage . . . the play's finest moments perfectly capture that inky almost emperceptibly agitated darkness just before the fences of racism, for a time, can crash down."—Frank Rich, *The New York Times.*　　(260485—$6.95)

☐ **IBSEN: The Complete Major Prose Plays, translated and with an Introduction by Rolf Fjelde.** Here are the masterpieces of a writer and thinker who blended detailed realism with a startlingly bold imagination, infusing prose with poetic power, and drama with undying relevance and meaning. This collection includes *Pillars of Society, A Doll House, Ghosts, An Enemy of the People, Hedda Gabler, When We Dead Awaken,* and Ibsen's six other prose plays in chronological order.
(257972—$14.95)

☐ **A WALK IN THE WOODS by Lee Blessing.** "Best new American play of the season" —Clive Barnes, *The New York Post.* A stunningly powerful and provocative drama, based on an event that actually took place . . . probes the most important issue of our time—the very survival of civilization.　　　(261996—$6.05)

Prices slightly higher in Canada

Buy them at your local bookstore or use this convenient coupon for ordering.

NEW AMERICAN LIBRARY
P.O. Box 999, Bergenfield, New Jersey 07621

Please send me the books I have checked above. I am enclosing $_____ (please add $1.00 to this order to cover postage and handling). Send check or money order—no cash or C.O.D.'s. Prices and numbers are subject to change without notice.

Name_____

Address_____

City_____ State_____ Zip Code_____

Allow 4-6 weeks for delivery.
This offer, prices and numbers are subject to change without notice.